YET NOT ALONE

YET NOT ALONE

The Story of Barbara and Regina

TRACY LEININGER CRAVEN

ZONDERVAN.com/
AUTHORTRACKER
follow your favorite authors

ZONDERKIDZ

Alone Yet Not Alone
Copyright © 2012 by Tracy Leininger Craven

This title is also available as a Zondervan ebook.
Visit www.zondervan.com/ebooks

Requests for information should be addressed to:
Zonderkidz, 5300 *Patterson Ave., S.E., Grand Rapids, Michigan* 49530

Library of Congress Cataloging-in-Publication Data

Craven, Tracy Leininger, 1978–
    Alone yet not alone / by Tracy Leininger Craven.
      p. cm.
    Summary: In 1755, in the Blue Mountains of Pennsylvania, sisters Barbara and Regina
    Leininger are carried away from their family by Allegheny warriors, but hold onto
    their faith in God and belief that they will one day be reunited.
    ISBN 978-0-310-73053-8 (softcover)
      1. Leininger, Regina, b. 1746? – Captivity, 1755–1764 – Juvenile fiction. 2. Leininger,
Barbara – Captivity, 1755–1759 – Juvenile fiction. [1. Leininger, Regina, b. 1746? – Captivity,
1755–1764 – Fiction. 2. Leininger, Barbara – Captivity, 1755–1759 – Fiction. 3. Indian
captivities – Pennsylvania – Fiction. 4. Indians of North America – Pennsylvania – Fiction.
5. Christian life – Fiction. 6. Pennsylvania – History – French and Indian War, 1754–
1763 – Fiction. 7. United States – History – French and Indian War, 1754–1763 – Fiction.]
I. Title.
PZ7.L53475Alo 2013
[Fic] – dc23
                                       2012015576

A true story of an American family torn apart, a young sister's faith in God, and her heroic and daring escape.

Editor: Kim Childress
Art direction and cover design: Kris Nelson
Interior design: Ben Fetterley and Greg Johnson/Textbook Perfect

Printed in the United States of America

12 13 14 15 16 /DCI/ 20 19 18 17 16 15 14 13 12 11 10 9 8 7 6 5 4 3 2 1

To my dearest love David and our three precious children, Elaina, Evangelina, and Wyatt. Each a constant source of joy. And in loving memory of my grandmother, Berneta Leininger, for her example of love and devotion to God and her family.

Contents

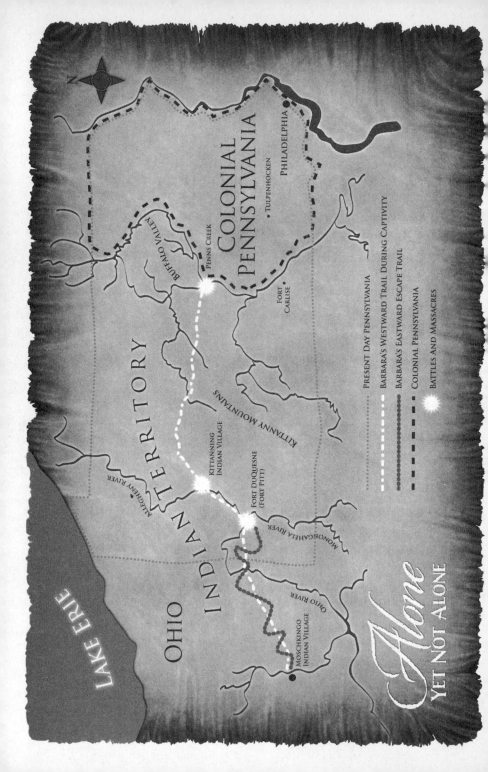

INTRODUCTION

*D*eep within America's vast frontier, nestled high among the Blue Mountains of Pennsylvania, was a lush green valley fringed on its southern border by Penn's Creek. Long before any settlers beheld its beauty or tilled the soil, the Indians named this fertile land Buffalo Valley.

Despite the wild country, a handful of families came to dwell there. They lived happily in harmony with both God and man — even with the Indians.

Barbara and Regina Leininger's family was among these few. They came across the sea from Germany to start a new life in America. They forged their way over the unmarked mountain ranges to the farthest outpost on the Pennsylvania frontier. With their own hands, they built a little log cabin nestled between two huge maple trees on a knoll overlooking Penn's Creek.

Each day they toiled tirelessly, never regretting comforts they had left behind or the rigors of the frontier life they had chosen. Tired though they were, their hearts were alive with spirit and full of thanksgiving to God for blessing them in their new homeland.

The fall of 1755 bestowed on the Leiningers' world not only its rich beauty but also a rewarding harvest. On this particular day the whole valley seemed to rejoice in the fullness of the season. The autumn sun settled in the western sky, illuminating the rich tones of the maple trees and lighting the valley with hues of crimson and gold. Its rays reflected in the creek's rushing water until it glistened and jumped like fire.

Dusk settled peacefully upon the Leininger family as they completed their day's work and prepared for the evening meal. Everything was as it had been the day before — everything, that is, except the dark-tanned figure as silent as one of the oaks crouching on the ridge that overlooked the creek. His clothing blended with the surrounding forest. His penetrating dark eyes watched the family's every move.

Chapter 1

END OF A PERFECT DAY

*B*arbara Leininger shielded her blue eyes from the sun as she looked up at the tall cornstalks that stretched high above her. Though she was tall for a twelve-year-old, Barbara felt far too short as she stood on her tiptoes to grab one last ear of corn. The sun began to sink low on the horizon, casting its rays on her golden hair.

"There!" she said to Regina, her nine-year-old sister, who stood with a half-filled apron. "Now we can head home and help Mama with dinner. And I'll even let you carry this juicy ear of corn." She placed the prized ear in her sister's homespun apron.

Regina's eyes sparkled with pleasure, and a mischievous smile played around her deep-pink lips. "Thank you kindly, sister," she said with a slight curtsy. Then, without a second's warning, Regina dashed through the field toward their cabin. "I'll race you back," she cried merrily over her shoulder.

Barbara, who always loved a challenge, was off in a flash. It didn't take long for her to catch up to Regina, but she held back, allowing her younger sister the pleasure of winning. They both arrived home breathless but laughing gaily, their eyes shiny and their cheeks rosy.

Their mother stood in the doorway of their little log cabin and greeted her daughters in German. "I see my girls have been hard at work today!"

As she picked the corn from their aprons, her kind eyes and loving smile warmed Barbara's heart.

"Run along now, and see if you can help your father."

Barbara took Regina's hand and led her around to the woodpile, where her father was chopping wood. With a determined blow, he split one last log. Then, burying the sharp ax in the old tree stump, he bent down to pat their German shepherd, Luther. In return, the dog wagged his tail furiously and licked his master's hand.

Barbara stooped down to gather small pieces of wood for kindling, but Regina stood with her eyes fixed on the horizon. Looking up, Barbara followed her gaze. John, their nineteen-year-old brother, emerged from the woods at the far end of the field. His musket was flung over his shoulder, and even from this distance, Barbara could see the wide grin on his face. When Barbara saw Christian, their oldest brother, who was twenty, she knew immediately why John was grinning. Two plump geese hung over his shoulder. Luther ran to meet them, barking loudly and jumping up to lick their faces.

"Thank heaven!" Mother Leininger cried. "They have returned home safely." The worry lines on her brow disappeared. "We will have meat with our dinner too!" She whispered a prayer of thanksgiving. The Lord had blessed another day's labor. Mother Leininger smiled and hurried back inside their cabin and to the hearth to finish dinner.

Soon the last glimmer of sun had faded beyond the western horizon, and the frontier family was serene in the comfort of their snug cabin. The light from the hearth cast a warm glow about them, softening each face. They shared the kind of family unity that comes from working together with one goal—not just survival in this sometimes hostile land, but of serving their Heavenly Master by walking in genuine love.

After their hearty supper, Barbara helped her mother clear the table. Regina snuggled between her two big brothers, listening intently as they told of their hunting adventures.

Barbara noticed Father look up from the old leather harness he was repairing with a gratified smile and look lovingly at each of his children, lingering a moment longer on Regina. Barbara knew Regina, the baby of the family, held a special place in all their hearts. Her childlike love for life, wild imagination, and animated personality both amused and endeared her to all of them. She was her mother's namesake and could not have been named better with her same chestnut brown hair and eyes as true a blue as the sea on a sunny day. Father always said Regina's eyes sparkled like the ocean just like her mama's eyes.

Barbara overheard bits and pieces of John's story as she scraped the leftovers into a dish for Luther, who lay at the hearth, wagging his tail and licking his jaws.

"I was sneaking through a thickly wooded riverbank," said John, "when, suddenly, I saw two—"

"John." Regina shook his arm frantically and her eyes grew wide in alarm. "What about the Indians? If you were in the woods all alone, an Indian might get you with his tomahawk." Silence filled the cabin. Even Luther cocked his head to the side and whimpered.

Barbara had heard the rumors. Unrest was growing between the French and the English over their western borders. Some said many Indian nations would ally with the French.

"Regina, Regina! My! What ideas your little head comes up with." John tousled his sister's hair affectionately. "You know the Indians are our friends. They sold us this land. Besides, there has not been an Indian raid in Pennsylvania since the colony first saw settlers over seventy years ago."

Despite John's reassuring words, Barbara noticed Mother glancing at Father with a concerned look. He paused, thinking deeply before he spoke. "Regina, do you remember why your mother and I decided to come to this land?"

"Yes, sir," Regina said smiling. "Because here we are slave to no man and are free to live as God sees best."

"That is right, my little one," Father said and then took Mother's hand in his. "When your mother and I decided to leave Germany to come to this land, we knew there would be dangers and hardships, but we also knew it was the price we must pay for freedom. Even if the Indians were to attack and take our lives, we would still be free. What could be more wonderful than to go from our beautiful valley straight to heaven?"

Christian, who had been deep in thought over the whole matter, added gravely, "Papa's right, Regina. I remember what it was like to till the count's land in Germany. We broke our backs working the fields, only to nearly starve during the long winters." He took a deep breath. "I would give my life any day to be here as a free man. Even though I cannot imagine it, heaven will be even more glorious than this."

"Regina, I think it is time for you to help your sister with the dishes," said Mother. Regina, who was never worried about anything for more than a moment, jumped up from her seat and skipped over next to Barbara at the washbasin.

As Barbara dried the last of the dishes, she could hear her father making plans for the following morning. Even though he sounded perfectly at peace, he was taking extra precautions.

"John," Father said, "your mother is going to the mill tomorrow to grind the harvested corn into meal, and as you know, it is a good day's journey." Looking squarely into John's face, conveying through his eyes more than he spoke, Father continued. "I will need Christian's help in the fields and I want you to go with your mother to the mill."

Father turned to Barbara just as she dried the last dish. Though he tried to hide his concern, Barbara saw the forced smile. "Come, my golden-haired princess, let us read the Scriptures."

Barbara blushed with delight at the compliment of being called her father's princess. Rushing to the old German trunk, which had traveled with them all the way across the ocean, she opened it and carefully lifted out the large Bible.

Father waited until the ladies had situated themselves about the table before opening the black cover with its beautiful gold lettering shining by the firelight. Then in his deep and caring voice, he began to read the words that melted away all the fears and cares of the day.

Barbara listened carefully to every word. She could tell Regina, who sat next to her, was trying her best to sit still. But her eyes darted about the room, her hands toyed with the tucks in her dress, and her foot kicked Barbara's leg in rhythm as if she were keeping time with the dog's wagging tail. It was evident that her mind had drifted far away into one of the lands where her vivid imagination often traveled.

Barbara nudged her little sister. Regina jumped in alarm and glanced at Father with repentant yet playful eyes and joined them in reciting their daily memory passage, Deuteronomy 8:2.

"'And thou shalt remember all the way which the Lord thy God led thee these forty years in the wilderness, to humble thee, and to prove thee, to know what was in thine heart, whether thou wouldest keep his commandments, or no.'" Father again looked lovingly around the snug room and whispered thanks to his Heavenly Father for the blessings that had been bestowed on them.

After a few thought-filled moments, he looked at Barbara and asked, "Do you know what that Scripture means when it talks about the Lord's taking his people through the wilderness?"

"Yes, Father." Barbara was pleased to know the answer. "It's talking about the children of Israel, after they left Egypt."

"That's right, my little princess." Father smiled approvingly. "But did you know that God led me through a similar wilderness?"

Everyone eagerly turned toward Father. They loved to hear him speak of the past, for he could tell stories better than anyone else.

"Yes, it too was a test of about forty years. It was to see if my heart would remain faithful to the Lord. You see, when I was a young man in Germany—about your age, John—I heard of a faraway promised land with fertile soil and rich with wild game. Unlike the count's crowded valley, which my family had farmed for generations, a man could live on his own land, make a living, and even have an inheritance to pass on to his children." Father stared into the dying embers in the hearth with a faraway look in his eyes.

"Naturally, I wanted to pack up and leave Germany right away, but God had other plans. No, before I could leave Germany, I needed to walk through some trials and tests. God knew the lessons I needed to learn before my faith was ready for this promised land." Father chuckled and shook his head. His hand ran over the dry, brittle leather of the harness he had been repairing. "At times the challenges were so difficult that I thought I would never make it. But now that I am here—in this wonderful place God promised—I can see it was the trials that prepared me for the blessings God had for us in this new country."

He looked gravely at his children and then with tender earnestness he went on. "Each of you will have times of testing in your life. But you must always remember—no matter how difficult the trial or how dense the wilderness—God will never leave you. If your hearts remain true, God promises endless blessings."

His words stirred Barbara's heart. The silence that followed was only interrupted by an occasional snap from the slowly vanishing embers. Mother began softly humming the tune of an old German hymn. Soon the whole family joined in, and they sang the comforting and rich words to "Alone, Yet Not All Alone."

Regina's voice carried above the others. She loved singing; mother always called her their little songbird. But of all the hymns, this was her favorite. Barbara smiled at her little sister as they sang verse after verse.

> *Alone yet not all alone am I*
> *Though in this solitude so drear*
> *I feel my Savior always nigh;*
> *He comes the weary hours to cheer*
> *I am with Him and He with me*
> *I therefore cannot lonely be.*

Father asked Christian to close with prayer, and then Mother suggested it was time for Barbara and Regina to be off to bed. Barbara let down the curtain that separated their sleeping area from the rest of the cabin and quickly changed into her long, woolen nightgown. The room was cold away from the hearth, so she could not wait to jump into bed with Regina. She was glad to share a bed, especially on cold nights. When they were ready, Mother pulled back the curtain and sat on the edge of their straw-ticked mattress. She pulled the covers up around Barbara's chin and bestowed a tender kiss on her forehead. Barbara yawned.

"Oh, please, Mother," whispered Regina with childlike affection, "will you sing my song once more?"

"Ah, but you must get to sleep, my little one. I can already see your eyelids are heavy. How will you grow tall and strong like Barbara if you never let them rest?"

"Yes, Mother, but I always dream sweetly when I fall asleep listening to the sound of your voice."

Mother laughed and then placed a kiss on Regina's

forehead. Her melodious voice filled the cabin with its soothing tones. Barbara watched as the last glow of fire-light flickered across her mother's pretty face. Her expression was so full of love and joy that Barbara's heart filled with an unexplainable peace. The dangers that lay in the forest beyond now seemed far away. Slowly, she drifted into sleep.

Outside, the tall figure, who just hours before had stood still as a statue watching the family, had long since sneaked back into the slumbering forest just as quietly as he had come. He now sat in front of his own campfire, his eyes burning as bright as the light that flickered before him. His face did not soften in the gleam, but instead the dancing reflection high-lighted his hardened features and accentuated the furrows in his brow. Soon his companions joined him, engaging in deep and agitated conversation until, at last, all was settled and they too fell asleep. Only, their dreams were of a different sort than Barbara's; they were not of peace and tranquility.

Chapter 2

CAPTURED!

*B*arbara awoke and dressed hurriedly as the earliest shades of morning stole across the eastern horizon. Darkness still surrounded their cabin and the morning star hung steadfastly in the sky, twinkling as if happy to be the only star still shining from the heavens. She shook Regina, who was still snuggled deeply under the warm patchwork quilt Mother had brought from Germany. It was a treasured wedding gift. "Hurry, Mother and John are leaving."

Regina rubbed her eyes and stretched. With a start, she sat straight up in bed. "Mother's leaving?"

"Yes, for the mill, remember?" Barbara laughed at her drowsy sister.

Regina bounded out of bed.

Their mother and John, already prepared for their day's journey, quietly bid the family good-bye as if they didn't want to break the tranquility of the morning.

Regina, however, made up for the quiet. "Good-bye, my dear mother," she said, throwing her arms around her neck. Barbara wondered if she ever intended to let go. Finally, Regina bounded off toward John and bid him a similar farewell.

Mother looked down at Barbara and brushed a strand of hair out of her eyes. "Take good care of Father and Christian while I'm gone. I've left some salt pork in the cupboard for stew." Mother smiled and hugged her daughter affectionately. "And if you can, see to it that Regina practices the spelling and arithmetic lessons on her slate while your father is in the field."

"I'll take good care of her, Mother." Barbara was delighted that her Mother treated her as if she were one of the grown-ups.

Having already bid them farewell, Father and Christian were headed for the barn to see to the livestock while Mother and John climbed into the wagon. Barbara held Regina's hand as the wagon, followed by Luther, who was merrily wagging his tail, headed down the trail. They watched until it blended in with the dim light of the morning.

Regina shivered and huddled closer to Barbara. With Mother gone, Barbara now took her place.

"Has the chill of the morning air nipped you?" Barbara asked, putting her arm around her little sister. "Don't worry. Our morning chores shall drive it away."

"It's not that I'm cold," answered Regina more to herself than to Barbara. "I was just thinking how I do not like good-byes." She gripped Barbara's hand tightly. "How awful it would be if I never saw Mother again."

"Regina, there goes your imagination again. Don't be silly! Besides, it's dreadful to dwell on such things. Mother and John will be home by lunch tomorrow." But Barbara shifted uneasily. She had already had the same thought as she watched the wagon disappear into the woods.

"Come," said Barbara. "Christian has promised to take us to the LeRoys' cabin after lunch if we complete all our chores this morning."

The LeRoys were a Swiss family that lived halfway across the valley. They were the Leiningers' nearest neighbors and shared the same faith and convictions. It was not uncommon for the two families to help with each other's workloads, especially during the harvest season. The girls looked forward to these visits because the LeRoys' only daughter, Marie, was about Barbara's age.

Delighted at the thought of visiting their neighbors, Regina was soon happily singing as she smoothed the bed quilts and swept the floor.

> *. . . He comes the weary hours to cheer*
> *I am with Him and He with me*
> *I therefore cannot lonely be . . .*

Barbara looked up from the corn she was shucking and watched Regina sing and dance around the corn-husk broom. "The hearth will never be clean at this rate." Barbara tried to hide the growing smile that threatened to encourage her sister's daydreamy behavior. "Do hurry,

Regina. It's almost time to start preparing lunch, and we still need to shuck and scrape all the corn we gathered yesterday."

"I can't wait to braid the dried husks into a rug!" cried Regina. "When do we start?"

"Not until the harvest is in and winter keeps us indoors. Then we can braid rugs, make new brooms, and even make cornhusk dolls!" Barbara unhooked the large iron kettle from the hearth and stoked the fire. It was time to start making the stew.

Barbara nearly flew from the cupboard to the table, to the hearth, and back to the table. Regina helped to chop the fresh carrots and potatoes she had gathered from the garden. Before they knew it, their father and Christian had returned from the field eager for the lunch the girls had carefully prepared. It wasn't often that their mother left Barbara in charge of the house, and she was determined to fix the finest meal possible for the men.

As it turned out, the stew tasted a little scorched and the rolls were not as light as Mother's, but both went unnoticed. The girls glowed with the praise they received from their father.

"Girls, your brother and I could not be more pleased with the lunch you have prepared," he said with a sideways glance and wink at Christian. "A man could never survive in this wilderness if—"

Suddenly, the cabin door swung open and in walked two Indian braves.

Christian and Father jumped to their feet and stood

face to face with the grim-faced warriors. Barbara blinked in disbelief. She had seen Indians before, but never had they stormed into the cabin in such a manner. Their dress was unfamiliar. They were mostly bald, except for a few eagle feathers attached to a tuft of hair in the center of their heads. Their faces were painted with stripes, hardening their sharp features and accentuating their sullen eyes. They wore several leather straps across their strong painted chests, and various weapons dangled from the straps. Barbara noted that their powder horns looked very much like Christian's, but other than that the implements were unfamiliar.

Looking at Father, Barbara immediately sensed his alarm. She watched in amazement as he quickly regained his composure. "Please sit and have some stew." Father gestured toward the table.

At first Barbara wondered why he had so quickly forgotten their startling behavior. But then she remembered John had said the Indians near their valley had always lived in peace. She reasoned that her father was just trying to assure the braves of his friendship.

Again her father motioned for them to take a seat, but the warriors stood silently surveying the room. The younger of the two stared at Barbara's blond hair as if he had never seen the like. Barbara shifted uneasily and put her arm around Regina, who had inched closer to her big sister.

After what felt like hours, the older brave pointed at Barbara and said, "Squaw, give whiskey!" The gaze from his cold eyes penetrated to her bones.

Father quickly answered for his daughter in a controlled yet firm voice. "We have no whiskey. Surely our Indian brother would like to smoke some tobacco instead." Knowing the Indians' love for tobacco, the Leiningers had stored away a stash for occasions like this.

The Indians grunted in reply. Barbara, thankful for an excuse to get away from their expressionless faces and piercing eyes, quickly motioned for Regina to follow her as she crossed the room to get the tobacco out of the trunk. Following the example of her father's boldness, she promptly returned to offer the Indians the tobacco.

The warriors seemed satisfied and sat by the hearth, quietly smoking a full pipe of tobacco. Father and Christian returned to the table and continued to eat their lunch, pretending not to be bothered by the odd actions of their guests. Regina and Barbara retreated to the far end of the cabin and sat on the edge of their bed, finding comfort in distancing themselves from the painted warriors. Regina sat close to her sister and stared blankly at the stripes on Barbara's apron.

Barbara studied the Indians more closely. The younger brave was definitely taller and stronger, but his eyes were not as fierce. He looked to be about John's age.

The other Indian was much older, by at least fifteen years. He also had a long hooked nose. His gruff mannerisms made Barbara more frightened of him. The older warrior carried a musket. A tomahawk hung from his belt. She noticed a peculiar object hanging next to it. Her heart surged with sudden horror as she realized what she was seeing. It appeared very much like she imagined a scalp would look. Barbara quickly closed her eyes, trying to wash away the thought.

Her father must have noticed the same thing because he calmly, yet urgently, spoke to the girls in German — a language the Indians could not understand. "Girls, go now to the creek and fetch some water — but you must not return until after the Indians have gone." The girls started toward the door, and he turned to the Indians and spoke in English, "You must be thirsty from your travels; the girls will go and get water."

Barbara quickly took Regina's hand and grabbed the watering pail. As the girls crossed the threshold, Barbara looked back.

The Indian with the long hooked nose abruptly stood and with fiery eyes declared in broken English, "We Allegheny Indians, friend of French." He narrowed his gaze. "Brothers no longer."

That was the last Barbara heard as she rushed out the door. She did not fully understand, but she knew something was dreadfully wrong.

Once outside, Barbara wanted to run to the creek and distance herself from the unwelcome visitors. But for Regina's sake, she made herself be strong.

"I don't like those Indians," Regina whispered. "Why do they carry so many weapons?"

"Maybe they've been hunting," Barbara suggested as they reached the creek bank. "I'm sure they will leave soon."

Barbara felt far more secure under the sheltering branches of the birch trees that grew along the water's edge. Holding up their skirts, they waded knee deep into the cool current so they could dip the bucket in the freshest water. Unfortunately, the feeling of safety did not last long. Within moments Barbara heard a terrifying whoop coming from the direction of the cabin, followed by a gunshot, then an eerie silence.

"Barbara," Regina whispered, "what ... what was that?"

Barbara looked down at her little sister. All the color had left Regina's rosy cheeks, and she was trembling like a maple leaf shimmering in the autumn winds. Taking Regina's hand, Barbara attempted to calm her fright, but she found that her own hand shook just as much.

Fastening her gaze into the shadows beyond the open cabin door, Barbara anxiously waited for her father to appear. There was nothing, no one, just silence. Without thinking, she let her wool skirt drop into the cold rushing waters.

Then the noise began. There was loud crashing and banging as if things were being tossed around the cabin. Wood splintered as if the dinner table was knocked over and the chairs broken to pieces. Barbara realized the Indians were plundering their cabin. Straining, she heard material ripping. Her eyes widened as bits of straw and cornhusks flew out of the door. Had they ripped open the bedding? Barbara could hear sparks snap and crackle as the hearth fire grew stronger. What were they burning?

It wasn't until black smoke began to billow out of the chimney and drift out through the doorway that Barbara saw the two Indians run into the yard. She instinctively urged Regina to hide among the tall grass. Soon dense smoke poured out of the door opening, causing Barbara to fear for her father's and brother's lives.

Why didn't they come out? She tried to see into the darkened cabin. It was then that she noticed the Indians were carefully surveying the yard, the barn, the cornfield beyond, and then the creek bank.

They were looking for them! She wanted to call for Father and Christian to come rescue them, but she knew they had to be quiet. Her heart ached to catch a reassuring glimpse of Father.

The Indians' penetrating gazes swept over Barbara and Regina's hiding place. Barbara put her arm around Regina, slowly pressing her deeper into the moist grassy bank. She held her breath and hoped they would pass over them. But the Indians' skilled eyes quickly picked out their forms among the grasses.

A few quick strides and the strong braves stood towering above the trembling girls. Barbara tried to scramble out of their reach, but the younger warrior grabbed her arm and yanked her to her feet. Twisting, Barbara turned toward the brave and kicked him with all the strength she could gather. He stood unmoved and appeared almost amused at her struggle.

Looking defiantly at the brave, she tried to yank her

arm free. "Where is Father?" she yelled. "I must get back to the cabin."

The older brave secured Regina under his arm and bolted for the shelter of the nearby forest. Stretching her arms back toward the burning cabin, Regina cried out in sheer panic, "Papa! Papa! Come get me, Papa!" Tears streamed down Regina's face as she watched her home disappear behind the dense trees.

"Regina!" Barbara cried as she saw her sister being carried into the woods. Barbara had to stop him. She had to save her sister. "Regina!" she cried again. Ceasing her struggle, she let herself be dragged away, toward her sister. The young brave had already tightened his grip on her arm, and with quick strides he also headed for the forest.

As Barbara stumbled along behind him, she caught glimpses of Regina's pale face and glints of the fierce warrior's tomahawk. Barbara struggled to keep up with her young captor's fast pace. She was determined not to let Regina out of her sight.

Chapter 3

THE PROMISE

*I*t was all Barbara could do to stay on her feet as the strong, young warrior dragged her through the forest. Barbara tried to free herself, but his grip on her wrist was unyielding, and he raced along with ease and agility. Her foot caught in a tangle of underbrush and blackberry vines. She tripped and fell, but the warrior's grasp did not weaken. The blackberry thorns shred her dress, and she felt cutting stings and fresh blood run down her legs as they ripped into her flesh. Barbara fought to scramble back to her feet only to fall again.

The Indian pulled Barbara up the ridge that overlooked their valley. She longed to look back at the cabin to see if there were any traces of Father and Christian, but she forced herself to keep her eyes straight ahead. She must not lose sight of Regina. Every so often Barbara caught flashes of her sister's red dress through the shadows of thick hemlock boughs.

At last they emerged into an opening at the top of the ridge. The brave loosened his hold on her, and she dropped at his feet. Then he joined a group of about twelve other Indians, who were talking excitedly among themselves.

Regina sat nearby, trembling and afraid to move from where the older brave had left her. Barbara inched her way over, closer to Regina, and wrapped her arm around her sister.

Regina's eyes filled with tears and her chin quivered as she buried her face in Barbara's shoulder.

Barbara gently smoothed her tangled hair. "Everything will be all right," she whispered. "Just wait. Father will not let them keep us forever." As she spoke she studied her surroundings. She could see the valley stretching out below and could hardly believe how far the Indians had already taken them. In the distance black structures dotted the valley. From each of them streaks of smoke funneled up into the sky. Her heart sank. Had the Indians burned their neighbors' houses too?

"There are so many," Regina whispered, almost too quietly to be heard. "But Papa will be here soon, won't he?"

Barbara looked at her sister, who sat wide-eyed and expressionless. She assured her with a slight nod and then gently wiped away the blood from a cut on Regina's cheek. But uncertainty gripped Barbara when she looked back toward the band of Indians. There were too many for Father and Christian to overcome by themselves. All the warriors were heavily armed, and their faces were decorated with what she assumed was war paint. Most of them wore similar clothing and spoke with the same accent as the Indian who had captured her, but some seemed to be from a different tribe. They did not wear the long leather leggings of her captor, and they communicated little with the others.

The brave who had dragged Regina up the ridge wore very little leg protection other than the moccasins that extended all the way up his calves and were fastened securely below his knees. Beads that bounced and danced with each little movement hung from the fringes at their tops.

Barbara saw that, though the Indians stood talking, their feet and legs never stopped moving. She could sense their restless excitement and feared what they would do next.

"Barbara!" Regina cried, pointing across the crude encampment. "Look! It's Marie!"

Near a large rock at the other end of the clearing, Barbara saw Marie huddled with several other children. She almost did not recognize her friend. Marie's shiny black hair was always neatly braided and fastened across the top of her head, but now it was matted and tangled. Marie glanced at Barbara and shook her head. Terror was written all over her pale, drawn face. For some reason Marie did not want to be recognized. "Shhh," Barbara whispered, gently placing her finger over her sister's mouth. Looking up, Barbara saw what Marie had feared—towering above them stood the older Indian with the long hooked nose.

"No speak in white tongue." The Indian glared down at Regina. "White father and brother dead—you Indian maiden—now speak Iroquoian, tongue of Allegheny master." The brave looked around at the other white captives who huddled in little groups about the camp. He wanted to make sure they all understood the meaning of his words. Then, as quickly as he had come, he strode away with a cold, hardened look.

Regina pressed her face into Barbara's lap and sobbed uncontrollably. Barbara's heart ached. She ran her fingers through her little sister's tangled hair as she tried to comfort her. The full gravity of their situation hit her, and tears welled up in her own eyes and unashamedly spilled below her long lashes. Father and Christian had not come out of the burning house. At first she had refused to believe they were dead. But now Barbara knew she would never again see them on this earth.

Before long, the braves gathered all of the captives together in a long line. Using coarse rawhide, they bound them by their wrists. The young brave who had captured Barbara came toward her and looked her straight in the eye.

She returned his gaze with courage.

His expression softened slightly, and he said, "I am Galasko, son of great Allegheny chief, brother of Hannawoa." He pointed to an older yet stoic looking brave who bore the marks of many battles. Galasko walked down the row of captives. His voice changed tones, hardening with each step. "I go with others and Hannawoa guards captives. He great warrior — keep many captives."

Galasko and the other braves collected their weapons and vanished into the forest. Hannawoa watched the captives carefully. His eyes were fierce and Barbara knew they missed nothing. He seemed like a coiled snake ready to strike at the slightest alarm. She found herself wishing Galasko had stayed instead.

Barbara longed to talk to her friend Marie, but she knew that was impossible. Marie's emerald green eyes, which normally sparkled with life, were now red and swollen, and her face, which almost always expressed lighthearted pleasure, was now tense and streaked with tears.

Barbara remembered the last time she had visited Marie, just over a week ago. Her friend had made a rich custard pudding as a surprise for Barbara and Regina. Marie had tried to keep it a secret until after dinner, but soon her dramatic, expressive personality had gotten the better of her, and she had laughingly told them about the pudding.

Marie glanced over at Barbara. A look of fear mixed with sadness passed between them. Barbara knew Marie's family must have experienced the same dreadful fate as Father and Christian.

The cry of a baby in the nearby woods, followed by the neigh of a horse, interrupted her thoughts. Before long three more warriors appeared; one was leading a horse. On it rode a beautiful blond woman who looked to be about Christian's age. The other two warriors carried a little boy and two girls about Regina's age. Finally, a fourth Indian appeared, carrying a crying child who looked about two years old. At the sight of the child, the young woman slid from her horse to the ground and fell to her knees. She cradled her hands over her heart as if she were rocking a child and wept.

"My baby! My baby! How could they—"

The brave who carried the little girl shoved the poor woman. For a moment Barbara thought the mother would be reunited with her child. But the frightened child shrunk away from both the brave and the crying woman.

"No speak white man's tongue or mourn death of white father's son. Your papoose too young to make long journey. White woman care for dead woman's child." He set the little orphaned girl in her lap.

The woman embraced the child and tried to soothe her fears, but her own sobs shook her entire body, and she silently mouthed, "My baby! My little baby," over and over.

Barbara watched in disbelief. The young woman must have been the wife of the young married English couple who had recently moved to the far end of the valley. She could only imagine a mother's grief at being torn from her baby, and she longed to comfort the woman. But Barbara looked down at the rawhide that cut into her wrists and knew there was nothing she could do.

All the next day and the day after that, they sat bound,

hand and foot, watching helplessly as more grief-stricken women and children were added to their group. Each evening the braves gave the captives small portions of coarse, dried meat and wild blackberries. Nevertheless, Barbara and the others awoke each morning with gnawing hunger pains and the knowledge that their next meal would not come until evening. Barbara prayed constantly for the raids to stop and for deliverance.

There was strength in numbers, she kept thinking to herself. And as long as they stayed in one place, the sooner help might come. By now Mother and John would surely have returned from the mill, and they would begin searching for them. Barbara knew John would not rest until she and Regina were safely home.

But no one came. Three days later the Indians awakened the party before dawn and forced them to begin a merciless march through the tangled underbrush of the forest. They walked at a brisk pace from dawn until dusk, pushing deeper and deeper into the heart of the Blue Mountains.

As each day passed, Barbara grew more and more concerned about Regina and wished she could help bear her sister's trial. Regina seemed too young and innocent to carry this burden. Barbara remembered how the fall colors normally warmed her sister's heart. The crisp air stirred her until she would squeal with sheer delight and skip and dance. But now, as Regina marched along in the solemn line of captives with her head hung low, she hardly took notice of the world around her.

Barbara, however, drew strength from observing the wondrous creation that surrounded them. The leaves above her looked like gold as they shimmered in streams of light that forced their way through the thick forest canopy.

"God makes *all* things beautiful in his time," Barbara whispered. She remembered the sound of her father's calm voice as he read the Scriptures to the family and how it had always soothed away the cares of the day. "Surely this trial is just for a season. All I need is the strength to endure — to see through the darkness of winter to the promise of spring." She remembered the long winter nights she and her mother had spent spinning flax and braiding rugs. Many times when Barbara had looked out at the bleak, white snow that covered any sign of life, she had wondered if spring would ever come. Mother had laughed and said the treasures of spring were God's precious gifts. The snow was merely his wrapping paper that kept them hidden until the right time.

"Our Heavenly Father knows we all love gifts, but we have to wait for his timing," she had said. "If we unwrapped the presents before the winter season is over, we could never appreciate them as much. Beneath the snow is dark, frozen dirt, but soon it will be rich, warm earth bursting with new life. His timing is always best."

Barbara longed for the warmth of their cabin and the tender voice of her mother. She watched the falling leaves and determined in her heart that she would not give up hope — she could make it through with Christ's strength.

It was evident that Regina did not hold the same hope in her heart. As each breeze grew colder so did her sister's fearful, saddened heart. She would do anything to see a smile return to Regina's lips and a merry twinkle dance in her eyes.

The terrain became totally unfamiliar and Barbara found Regina looking wistfully over her shoulder as if this was all a nightmare and she would wake up to find the valley she called home. Then, with sadness and fear spreading over the tender features of her face, Regina would look deep into her older sister's eyes for reassurance.

Even though she did not always feel it herself, Barbara tried to convey strength and hope to Regina. At night Barbara whispered the words of Regina's favorite hymn to her and prayed they would be a comfort. But when Regina just lay silent and unmoving in the darkness, Barbara's concern for her grew.

After five days of penetrating the vast and what seemed like endless forest, the Indians finally slowed their pace and eventually stopped to rest. That evening the braves gave the tired band of captives their meager allotment of dried meat and then allowed them to bed down early for the night. The braves sat around their campfire, immersing themselves in active conversation. Barbara watched their hand motions and facial expressions in the firelight. They were apparently boasting of their success.

As the moon rose higher in the stillness of the night, Regina dared to speak for the first time since the day they were captured.

"Barbara," Regina whispered so low she could hardly be heard. "What—what do you think they will do to us?"

"I'm not sure, Regina." She wrapped her arms around her little sister. "But, I know one thing—we are together, and I'll never let them take you away."

A tear ran down Regina's cheek and her voice quivered. "Do you—do you think we will ever see Mother again?"

Barbara gently ran her fingers across her sister's anxious brow while she tried to choke down the lump that was forming in her own throat. Then, sounding much more confident than she felt, she said, "Yes dear, we *will* see her again. Until then, we must be brave girls and remember what she and Father taught us. God will always be with us—even in our most difficult trials." They were silent for a moment. "The Indians may have taken us away from our home, but they can never take away our faith in Jesus Christ—no matter what happens. Even if something were to happen to me, never forget that God is with you." She looked at her sister in the moonlight. Barbara's lips quivered a bit and a tear ran down her own cheek. "Regina, do you remember how Mother calls you her little songbird? Promise me you'll never lose the song in your heart—no matter what happens."

Barbara's words seemed to stir Regina's heart. For the first time since they were captured, she smiled. Regina began to whisper the words to her favorite song, "Alone, yet not all alone am I ..."

Barbara hoped and prayed Regina would fully grasp

the words of the song and would find the comfort she needed. These Indians could take them away from everything and everyone they knew, but they could not take them away from their Savior. They would never be all alone!

Regina wrapped her arms around Barbara's neck. "I promise I will never forget—I will never lose the song in my heart."

Barbara watched as Regina fell into an exhausted slumber.

Chapter 4

I MUST ESCAPE

*B*arbara awoke early from a fitful night's sleep. Frost covered the ground. She snuggled closer to Regina, trying to warm herself. Soon the first glimmer of morning light crested the hills on the eastern horizon. Barbara tried to move the rawhide that bound her wrists to a less tender place.

The Indian warriors were already moving about the camp. Galasko quieted the black mare he had taken from Marie's farm. He spoke gently to the horse while he slipped the bit into her mouth and secured the bridle about her ears. Several of the other Indians had stolen horses too, but Galasko was the kindest master. Barbara had observed that his brother, Hannawoa, treated his horses with a quick, angry hand. Though he always had the horse under his control, the skittish behavior of the animal and the fear that burned in its eyes showed that it obeyed out of fear and not loyalty.

Barbara had named the Indian who had captured Regina Hook Nose. The Indians called him Mininka, but Barbara preferred her name for him. He had made her uneasy from the very first day, and she was sure he was the one who killed her father. Added to her disapproval of this man was that Hook Nose treated his horse in the worst way. When Hook Nose had first appeared with the polished bay mare, she had been as sure-footed and agile as the other horses. But after a few days of hard travel and Hook Nose's neglect, the horse began to founder. Now Barbara watched as he mercilessly forced the animal to accept a foal's bridle. The bit cut into the horse's mouth. Barbara knew that by the end of the day the mare's mouth would be raw and sore.

Hook Nose noticed Barbara watching him. She shifted uneasily and looked at the ground. Now that she had observed his heartless ways, she knew he was a bitter man who had even less compassion for the captives than he had for his horses.

Barbara dared to look up only when she heard footsteps approach. For a moment her heart stopped beating, but when she saw that it was Galasko, she let out a sigh of relief. Even Regina seemed to relax next to her, but when Galasko grasped the knife at his belt, she hid her head behind Barbara's shoulder. The young brave grabbed Barbara's hand and in one quick stroke cut the rawhide that bound her wrists.

"Many moons away from white man's village. Too far for white children to run. Now you will become Indian children—make good squaws and braves," he said, as he loosed the bonds from Regina and the others.

Barbara couldn't believe her hands were actually free from bondage. Adrenaline surged through her veins. She knew they could escape with the Lord's strength. All she had to do now was to wait for the right time. Barbara took Regina's hand in hers and squeezed it. She saw that Regina shared her sense of renewed hope—not only because her hands were free, but her heart seemed free too. All morning Regina had mouthed the words of her favorite song:

> *Alone yet not all alone am I*
> *Though in this solitude so drear*
> *I feel my Savior always nigh . . .*

It wasn't long before the braves were ready to press on. Barbara soon realized they were traveling faster now that her hands were free. Surely she and Regina could make it home in half the time it had taken to get this far west. All morning Barbara watched for an opportunity for flight, but soon she grew disheartened—escaping would be a greater challenge than she had anticipated. It seemed as if the braves could read her thoughts. They watched her with more intense scrutiny than before.

Many days had passed since the raid and the autumn tones were now faded. A chilly wind swept through the trees until the remaining leaves were finally unable to hold on any longer. Barbara watched as they fell to the ground and it saddened her heart.

"It is almost as though the beautiful leaves have lost all hope and have let go of the nourishment from their roots," she whispered to Regina, who was walking next to her.

Regina sighed and looked at the forest floor, which was thickly blanketed with a mixture of dead pine needles and faded maple leaves. "I must not give up—must never forget the God of our fathers—never lose the ..."

Barbara was relieved to see the change in her sister. She wrapped her arm around Regina's shoulder to convey the strength and assurance that at times Barbara was not even sure *she* possessed. From the beginning, she knew she had to act stronger than she felt, for Regina's sake. Many times Barbara wondered if she would have the same motivation and courage if something were to happen to her little sister.

About noontime, the Indians stopped at a spring to allow the weary band to rest and refresh themselves with the cool water. Barbara had just cupped her hands to drink from the rushing spring when she noticed Galasko arguing with Hook Nose. He gestured toward Regina and then Barbara. Galasko shook his head with firm determination. Barbara could tell something was dreadfully wrong. She had not seen Hook Nose look so angry. Barbara protectively placed her hand on Regina's shoulder as the braves' heated conversation continued for a few anguishing moments. Barbara's mind raced as she tried to guess what kind of trouble loomed ahead.

With a few long strides, Galasko made his way briskly

across the camp, grabbed the small two-year-old girl out of the English woman's arms, and returned to Hook Nose. They continued arguing for several more minutes. Finally, with a grunt of dissatisfaction, Hook Nose pointed at the little girl in Galasko's arms, then to Regina, and then to himself. They had come to an agreement over something, and Barbara was not sure she would like the conclusion.

Galasko strode over to Regina and handed her the child. "This your baby now," he said. Then he pointed at Hook Nose. "You go with Mininka, to his village, and you ..." He turned to Barbara, smiled, and held a strand of her golden hair up to the sunlight. Then he reached for her arm. "You now Susquehanna; name mean White Lily. You come to village of my fathers."

Barbara's heart froze. She stood still for a moment, and then abruptly pulled away from Galasko. "No," she cried, wrapping both her arms around Regina and the child in her arms. "I will *not* leave my sister!"

One of Galasko's braves raised his tomahawk and threatened Barbara. But Galasko held out his hand and motioned for the brave to halt. He grabbed Barbara's arm with one hand and secured his own tomahawk in the other. He motioned for her to follow. Barbara resisted. She would not go with him. She could not leave her sister — especially with Hook Nose. She looked from Galasko to the brave standing nearby, whose weapon was still raised, ready to take action if Barbara refused to obey.

She glanced at Regina. Her face was pale and she trembled at the sight of the brave's tomahawk. Barbara's protective instinct told her she must stay with her sister, but reason told her to submit. To resist now would be certain death. But if she gained their trust through compliance, she would have a better chance of escaping later.

Softening her resistance, Barbara whispered one last thing into Regina's ear. "Remember your promise."

Galasko pulled her away.

It was all Barbara could do to make herself follow him to a nearby horse. As Barbara mounted, she noticed Galasko had four Indian braves under his command. They stood like a giant, unyielding wall between her and her sister.

Much confusion followed as the braves divided the captives into different parties. It became clear to Barbara that the warriors were separating them according to their village or tribe. Galasko grabbed Marie and put her on the black mare.

Hannawoa whooped and said something about the Yengees just before he and a few other men headed back east. They did not take any of the captives.

Why did he not accompany Galasko? Was he going to join their French allies? Barbara knew *Yengees* was their term for the English colonials, and she hoped that he and his men were not going back to raid more settlers.

After everyone was divided up, Galasko took the reins of Barbara's horse and began to lead her away. Behind her followed Marie and the four other braves, who watched their every move. Barbara turned, trying to get a glimpse of her sister. She had never felt as helpless as she did while

Galasko led the party out of the clearing and onto the thickly wooded deer path beyond.

Regina stood in silent anguish, holding the small child whose little arms clung around her neck. Barbara watched as they slowly disappeared from view. She caught one last look in her dear little sister's eyes. Within them appeared deep sadness, yet the grief seemed mixed with hopeful promise — the promise that she would never forget her older sister's words. Barbara's eyes filled with tears until all was a blur.

Galasko looked back at her with disappointment. "Susquehanna not cry. She strong like mighty river — steady like a rock."

Barbara knew he would never understand and so she strove to hide her tears. She did not want him to see her grief. Wrapping her legs around the horse's back, she leaned forward, pretending to dodge the overhanging branches. She buried her face in the horse's cream-colored mane. Once her face was completely hidden, the tears flowed freely and she prayed under her breath, "Dear Lord, please let me see my dear Regina again." She tried to swallow the lump in her throat. "But no matter what happens, Lord, please let her never, never forget you."

Galasko did not like to see his Susquehanna lose the light in her eyes. Tears were a sign of weakness, so he was glad to see she had quickly regained her composure. "She is still young," he muttered in Iroquoian. "Soon she will forget her sadness and be happy to live in the village of my father." He picked up the pace, pressing farther and farther away from the spot where Barbara had last seen Regina.

Since the first day of her capture, Barbara had carefully observed the Indians. She already possessed a keen understanding of her master's temperament. The fact that he allowed the girls to ride the horses while the braves went on foot proved he underestimated her resolve to escape. With controlled strength, Barbara sat back on her tawny horse, pretending complete submission. She wanted Galasko to believe she had given up hope of ever again seeing her sister. All the while Barbara's mind raced, devising a plan for flight.

When the sunlight began to lazily filter through the trees, bringing deep evening shadows across the forest floor, Barbara saw her chance. It was obvious that Galasko felt there was no need to fear her escape because he had let go of the reins. This freed him to plow through the tangled vines and forest growth at a faster pace. Soon his thoughts were totally enveloped in the endeavor. Two of Galasko's braves followed directly behind their leader, while the two Indians at the back of the line, behind Marie and Barbara, argued in agitated tones over some animal signs along the trail that perplexed them greatly. Every so often they would kneel down and trace a deer print with their fingers or study a broken twig.

Barbara's heart raced. Up ahead there was a slight clearing in the brush that, if timed correctly, would give her the room she needed to turn her horse. Her cheeks flushed with determination as she tried to get Marie's attention. When Marie finally understood what Barbara's plan was, she looked petrified with fear and shook her head. Barbara knew this might be her only chance. She hated to leave her friend, but she had to find Regina before it was too late.

She jerked her horse's reins to the right and jabbed him with her heels. He turned, darted past the two braves behind them, and raced back down the heavily wooded path. Again, Barbara jammed her heels into his sides. With a snort and toss of his head, he lurched into a full gallop.

The wind whipped a strand of hair into Barbara's eyes, but she hardly noticed. All she felt was the exhilarating hope of freedom. If she could just make it a mile back to the creek, she could follow it for a while to hide her tracks. Barbara knew they had traveled west all day, so if she just headed away from the sunset, she would gain ground. She glanced over her shoulder to see if the braves pursued her. The next thing she knew, an overhanging branch hit her soundly on the shoulder, sweeping her off the horse's back. The fall would have been broken by the soft carpet of golden leaves, but Barbara's head hit a rock and she was knocked out cold.

When she awoke, her head hurt and all was a blur. Slowly her eyes made out the forms of two warriors. One held a blazing torch while the other grasped a stolen German Bible. Barbara saw that Galasko was not one of them.

What had happened? Where was Marie? Surely this was only a strange dream? Barbara tried to rub the swollen knot on her head, but she realized that both her hands and feet were tied to a young maple tree. Why had she been bound to a tree? What was happening?

"Read book of white man's God for last time." One of the braves sneered in her face as he held the Bible in front of her. "You die for running away." Everything came back—her capture, saying good-bye to Regina, her fleeing down the trail. This must be her punishment. Barbara felt numb.

Where was Galasko? Did he know what was happening? Her eyes searched the surrounding forest. He would save her. But Galasko was nowhere to be seen. Barbara looked back at the braves in front of her. Their eyes burned with loathing revenge.

Nervous beads of sweat dripped from Barbara's brow. Closing her eyes, she prayed for deliverance and the strength to endure with courage. The torch came so close to the pile of leaves at her feet that she could feel the intensity of the heat. Barbara looked heavenward.

"Lord, please forgive all my sins and give me strength to die with—"

"Wait!" a strong, firm voice called out in Iroquoian. Galasko broke through the shadowy woods. "I will speak with Susquehanna before you light the fire."

Chapter 5

THE BRITISH ARE COMING

W hy Susquehanna leave Indian brother?" Galasko demanded. "Has Galasko's hand not fed and cared for you?"

At first Barbara thought it odd that Galasko would be so indignant. Then she realized he had indeed been kind to her, and that she was extremely fortunate to have fallen into Galasko's hands rather than the other braves'.

"Please, Galasko, you have been a good master. It is not you that I run from. I only search for my sister. Please! Please let me live."

Galasko grunted with dissatisfaction. "With my people, you die for running away—must forget white sister. She now Delaware. You Allegheny. Bad to run. You make good wife for Indian warrior."

Barbara shrank away at the thought of becoming the wife of an Indian brave, but his words gave her hope. Maybe that meant he would let her live — give her a second chance. She wished she could read his thoughts, but Galasko appeared to be unmoved as he stood silently watching Barbara. His face was completely expressionless, and, though his eyes were fixed on her, they seemed indifferent as if he completely overlooked the pitiful end that awaited her. Barbara had not seen this side of her young master and began to fear the worst.

Finally, with a motion of his hand and some sharp words to the braves, Galasko ordered that she be released. The angry braves argued bitterly, but Galasko stood undaunted and quickly cut Barbara loose. Grabbing her by the arm, he led her away from the frightful and confusing scene to a grove where Marie was waiting beside the horses. Her feet and hands were tied together to keep her from running away. Galasko unbound Marie and ordered her to mount her horse.

He turned and glared at Barbara, and even though she did not understand the language, she knew from the tone of his voice and his piercing eyes that she was receiving a harsh scolding. It penetrated to the core of Barbara's being and placed within her a fearful respect for her master.

In his broken English, he said, "Warriors angry at white squaw — now angry at Galasko." He paused and thought for a moment. Then his eyes grew intensely fierce. "If Susquehanna leave again," he said, anger steeling his words, "she *will die*."

His declaration sent chills up her spine, and Barbara knew she would never forget it. A number of days passed before Galasko forgot his anger toward her. Barbara did everything she could to meet his approval and hoped he would once again treat her with kindness. Eventually he did, and before long Galasko became so lenient that he did not seem to mind if she and Marie spoke in English from time to time. When the other braves harshly disapproved, Galasko would encourage Barbara and Marie to use the Iroquoian tongue. He taught Barbara many words and even smiled in approval at her progress.

Soon autumn winds changed to the chill of winter. They traveled through the harsh winter snows until what Barbara surmised was mid-December. When the worn-down party was welcomed into the Indian village of Kittanny, it seemed as if they had finally reached their destination. The settlement rose from both the eastern and western banks of the Allegheny River.

Galasko spoke to her in Iroquoian and then explained in English. "Village of my father beyond setting sun. We stay here with tomahawk in hand. When French brothers drive away Yengee white man, we return to Galasko's village."

Barbara surveyed the village before her with mixed feelings. Marie also looked a little unsettled. Barbara took her friend's hand in her own and tried to be positive. "It will be good to have shelter during the winter months."

"Yes, this is true, but I wonder how the tribe will treat us. We will have to accept their way of life, but will they accept us?" Marie looked about her with uncertainty.

"Up to now our only concern was Galasko, and he seems pleased with almost anything *you* do, but now there is a whole tribe to please."

Barbara dismissed the thought of Galasko's treating her with special kindness and studied her new surroundings. Much to her relief, she saw they were not the only white captives. Everywhere she looked Barbara saw pale faces — both women and boys intermingled with the tanned complexions of the Indians. Most seemed glad to see them, but their happy expressions were mixed with pity. Barbara sensed they were afraid to acknowledge Marie and her, but she understood. They feared the Indians' disapproval. That would soon wear off; Barbara was sure of it.

She was glad to rest from what had seemed like endless travel, but life in this crude village appeared grim. The white captives were gaunt and weak from their labors, and almost all the villagers looked as if they suffered from the harsh effects of the long cold winter months.

Smoke funneled out of small openings in the roofs of countless roughly assembled long houses. There were very few braves, and Barbara concluded that they must be either hunting game or fighting the English colonials. As she and Marie passed through the village, they noticed the older women sewing moccasins or deerskin pants for the men and knee-length skirts for the women. Their stoic faces changed very little as they worked. The younger women, who were skinning freshly killed animals or hanging strips of venison, paused to look up at them with curiosity. Barbara tried to catch their eyes, to see if they held any hint of friendship, but the Indian women would look away in shyness and uncertainty. The young children seemed the most curious and the most welcoming. Many of them would stop scraping their beaver hides and smile with fascination at the newcomers.

"Barbara!" Marie grabbed her hand and spoke in a mixture of Iroquoian and English. "Do you recognize that woman at the far end of the clearing?"

Barbara saw a young woman with blond hair that fell about her delicate facial features. She was struggling to pull a large pine branch out of the forest. Her thin build seemed far too small for the task. She looked familiar, but Barbara could not remember why.

"I am almost sure that is the same lady captured from Penn's Creek who lost her baby," Marie said.

Barbara remembered how sorry she had felt for the woman. She studied her more closely as the young lady drew near. Much to her amazement, she began to think Marie was right. But it did not seem possible. How had they ended up at the same village? Suddenly, a ray of hope began to warm Barbara's heart. If this woman could end up in the same village, maybe Regina could too. Maybe Regina was already here. Barbara decided she must talk with this woman at the first possible moment.

A number of days passed before Barbara could speak with the woman. She quickly learned she *was* the same person,

Lydia. She told Barbara she had not seen Regina since the day they were separated.

"Do take heart, though; many captives have passed through here. You might find your sister yet," Lydia said with a strong British accent. "Until then you will have plenty of work to keep your mind occupied." Lydia's face sobered and Barbara saw tears glistening in her soft brown eyes. "I have found that the only way for me to survive my own loss is to focus on doing the next thing and pray that we will be rescued."

Barbara smiled. She liked that. Do the next thing. She was grateful that she had met the kind English woman. Barbara knew they were kindred spirits.

Lydia was right; the days did seem to pass more swiftly when she focused on each task at hand. The workload was so heavy that she hardly found time to think of anything else; every hour of daylight was full. From dawn to dusk Barbara and Marie labored alongside the Indian women, tanning hides, chopping down trees for huts, and clearing the land for spring crops. At first the work seemed unbearable and each task was an unfamiliar challenge. But Lydia lent a helping hand and taught them everything she had learned. In addition, Barbara and Marie cooked and washed for Galasko and his four braves. Finding their own food, however, was not easy. They were allowed to eat any leftovers, but the summer's drought had crippled the corn crop and the winter snows were harsh. Many days the braves returned from a hunt with only a small porcupine or grouse. Often, this left

Barbara and Marie with empty stomachs. Their only hope for food was quick foraging jaunts into the woods, and those produced but a meager amount of acorns and tender roots.

"Only desperate hunger could make such food palatable," Barbara said to Marie one afternoon as she stooped to dig for grubs. "How I miss the taste of salt and freshly cooked meat."

"So do I," Marie agreed. With a faraway look in her eyes, she said, "I remember when my mother used to make fresh-baked custard every Sunday. It was my favorite. Now, it's even hard to remember the taste."

Despite the lack of food, Barbara began to grow more grateful that they had not traveled deeper into the western wilderness. She knew the farther they traveled, the less chance she had to someday escape. As the months passed, she understood more of the Iroquoian language. She and Marie heard much talk of the war with the British colonials. Often, Barbara would look back east, across the Allegheny River and past the long houses on the eastern side of the village. She hoped that someday soon this Colonel Armstrong, of whom the Indians so often spoke, would come from over the Blue Mountains and rescue them.

Soon winter melted into the freshness of spring, and hope flourished within Barbara's heart. Each day as she cleared land for spring planting, she would longingly gaze at the eastern mountains and listen for any sign of Colonel Armstrong and his men.

She was beginning to understand the Indians' way of life and what they expected from her. As the time for spring planting drew near, Barbara listened with fascination as an old Indian woman shared their tribe's ancient knowledge of how to grow corn. First, she soaked the plump kernels in a secret mixture of boiled herb juices. Then she explained in Iroquoian why their people were known throughout the land for producing the best crops. "After the cornstalk breaks through the earth and reaches up to the heavens, we plant beans and pumpkins around each base. They are the 'Three Sisters.' They help each other to grow strong and bear much fruit. The corn invites the beans to grow up its tall stalk, and the pumpkin spreads out her vines to choke out the weeds. The corn and the beans give nourishment to the soil and help their sister pumpkin plant to grow big and strong."

Smiling, Barbara stooped down, scooped up a handful of the rich soil, and smelled the fresh scent. Barbara remembered how each spring she and Regina had laughed and played together during planting season. At the end of the day they would have so much dirt on them that Mother would tease them, saying they had better leave some soil in the garden if they expected anything to grow. Barbara's eyes drifted back east and she sighed — she would have to remember to tell Mother and Regina about the "Three Sisters." Maybe John had already rescued Regina. She and Mother might even be praying for Barbara's return at this very moment. Surely it was just a matter of time before the great English colonel would come and she would be free to return to her family.

But the spring corn she had planted grew high in the hot summer haze and then yellow with the coming of the harvest sun. Barbara wondered if the British were ever coming. Perhaps the rumors were not true. Barbara feared the French and Indians had overpowered the British colonel her master feared so much.

Late one afternoon in early autumn, Barbara was near the water's edge, grinding corn into meal on a flat rock. She heard rapid gunfire coming from the opposite end of the village on the eastern side of the Allegheny River. The Indian braves answered with piercing war whoops. The large stone she held fell aimlessly to the ground as the gunfire and terrifying war whoops echoed across the river. Barbara resisted the urge to run. Instead she stood and quietly, slowly moved behind a large oak tree.

Could this be the colonel and his troops she had prayed for all these months? She tried to calm her excited anxiety as she peered around the tree. When she could see across the river without being noticed, Barbara crouched motionlessly and listened intently to the commotion. It was so near, yet she feared it was far—too far away. Finally, she heard the Indians crying out that the Yengees were ambushing them.

It *was* the English! Barbara's heart beat with wild excitement. They had come at last! Just then Barbara caught a glimpse of a British redcoat through the thicket. The thought of being rescued after one long year of being a slave seemed all too wonderful. Tears of hope and joy trickled down her tanned cheeks.

Once her hopes had climaxed, reality began to sink in. The soldiers were still on the other side of the river, and her freedom would not be secured unless the English overpowered the braves on both sides.

Suddenly, Barbara sensed she was not alone. A strong hand clasped her shoulder, jolting her back to the reality of her plight. Her heart sank as she turned to find herself facing Galasko.

"We must flee!" he said with an unyielding determination, completely indifferent to the sufferings of his fellow Indians across the river. Then Galasko muttered in Iroquoian, more to himself than anyone, "I would fight the white dogs myself, if I was not afraid of losing you." With fierce intensity she had seen before in his eyes, he said in English, as if to ensure that she understood his words, "We go hide in forest. Try to escape and you die."

Galasko grabbed her and rushed toward the dense undergrowth where he had already assembled Marie and the others. He gave his braves several terse instructions, and then they were off. Barbara raced after them; she knew if she attempted to slow her pace, the punishment would be too great to bear.

Chapter 6

THE LAND OF HIS FATHERS

The Indians led the captives over ten miles deeper into the wilderness before they stopped and made camp for the night. One brave went back to Kittanny as a scout. The next morning he returned with five broken-down and defeated warriors. They informed them that the British had overtaken and burned the village to the ground.

Barbara caught her breath. With them was Lydia, the young English woman. Her hair was tangled and her face was cut and bruised. Lydia's hands were bound and the braves declared that she must bear the punishment for an unpardonable crime. During the raid, she had tried to escape.

Barbara's heart was gripped with fear. She looked at

Marie, hoping to get assurance that everything would turn out fine. But Marie responded with a stunned, bewildered look. Barbara anxiously watched the braves counsel among themselves. After some time, horrifying war whoops filled the air. Barbara did not even want to imagine what would happen next. But she knew Lydia would be burned at the stake. She could feel the blood drain from her face, and her knees felt weak.

Barbara never forgot the scene that followed. With tears streaming down her face, she thanked God that Lydia was one of his children and prayed that he would take her home quickly and that her pain would be brief. Barbara longed to turn her face and hide her eyes from such dreadful brutality. But the angered warriors demanded that she and the others watch — they must witness the punishment they too would bear if they chose to forsake their Indian masters. Even Galasko said there was nothing he could do. Lydia was not his slave, and the laws of his people must be kept.

The warriors' plan was to frighten Barbara by making her watch the torture, but it only served to fuel the burning desire within her to be rid of the heartless laws and customs of this band of lost souls.

After they had carried out their punishment, Galasko ordered his party to journey to a land far beyond the western mountains where no white man dared to settle — the land of his fathers. On the way, they passed through many Indian villages. Barbara wondered if their journey would ever end. With each passing day, her hope of being rescued by the English army grew dimmer until she thought it would be useless to hope any longer. Yet Barbara still took note of different streams and mountain ridges and tried to remember them as landmarks in case she ever did escape. But soon the hills and rivers blended together, making her feel small compared to the endless wilderness that completely surrounded her.

Though time and miles passed, Barbara never lost the hope of somehow being reunited with Regina. At every village, she searched the faces of the white captives, hoping to find her sister. She even dared to speak to some, hoping they might have word of Regina's health or whereabouts. Still, there was no sign.

Just before winter set in, the little band of Indians climbed into a sturdy elm bark canoe and paddled across the Allegheny River to Fort Duquesne. This French fortification was strategically situated on the tip of a peninsula surrounded on two sides by the Allegheny and the Monongahela Rivers. The two rivers joined there and formed the mighty Ohio.

"We stay the winter here with French brothers," Galasko said. He looked at Barbara. "Winds tell of long, cold days to come. Susquehanna live here until spring rains."

Life within the sturdy walls of Fort Duquesne was bursting with activity. Frenchmen dressed in their regimental blue and white uniforms and Indians in their buckskins sat in the courtyard, talking around campfires and boasting of their mighty deeds. Women stopped washing clothes and looked up from the large iron kettles used as washbasins to examine the newcomers. Barbara could not help but smile as their children peered out from behind their mothers' skirts, too curious to hide yet too shy to come out. She could hear the clank of a hammer on an anvil as a blacksmith pounded out what Barbara assumed to be a horseshoe.

She could hardly believe how many stockades and people could fit within the fort. Its oddly shaped fortification walls jutted out and then angled back to form a star-shaped interior. Nearly six hundred French soldiers and one hundred Indian braves were there. Galasko said warriors from all of the tribes in the Band of the Six Indian Nations had come to support the French. He grunted when he saw some Delaware braves. "Delaware weak like women. They cowards."

In the past, Barbara had heard other warriors speak of the Delaware and wondered what they had done to merit such disdain. But this time there was only one thing on her mind. Hook Nose had taken Regina and he was a Delaware. Barbara immediately looked into the faces of the other white captives, hoping beyond hope to find her sister. After a day of careful searching, her heart sank. Once again, she saw no sign of Regina. Barbara looked down at her darkly tanned arms and toyed with her dyed brown hair. If it were not for her blue eyes, she would look just like an Indian. She wondered if Regina's captors had dyed her skin with black walnut juice too.

"Are you thinking of Regina again?" Marie whispered as she put her arm around Barbara's shoulders.

"Yes." Barbara sighed. Picking up a loose strand of her hair, she said, "You know how often I wonder where she is and hope that, if she is not already home, God has provided her with a friend like you. I do not know what I would do without your companionship. Regina is so young that sometimes I fear she will become accustomed to Indian beliefs and forget to trust in her Savior!"

"Barbara, you are such a good sister. Your prayers have been so fervent that I feel sure God will answer them. Do not lose heart. One day you will see her again." Marie took Barbara's hands in her own and tried to sound confident. "We must keep praying for Regina," she said. "And, we must pray that our own faith will not falter until we are free."

Barbara was grateful that Marie understood. Every day she thanked God for her friend. Both of them had now passed their thirteenth birthdays. The year they had spent together had so united them that they were able to read each other's thoughts.

"Thank you, Marie." Barbara squeezed her hand. "Together, with Christ's strength, we will continue on until we are free." She looked around her. The walls of the fort were guarded at every point with armed sentinels. At first, she had hoped the French would take pity on them and help them escape, but they were just as heartless as her captors. After just one day, she learned she could abide among the Indians far more easily than she could live among the proud, arrogant French soldiers. She could not wait until they moved on in the spring. They could never escape from these walls.

It did not take long for Barbara and Marie to settle into their daily chores. They worked for the French washing clothes, baking bread, and carrying water from the river. In exchange for their work, the French gave Galasko gunpowder and supplies. Many times Galasko would leave with a hunting party or scouting party and would not be seen for days. Whenever he was gone, many of the Frenchmen would try to convince Barbara to forsake her Indian master and stay with them when Galasko left the fort in the spring. She could not bear the thought of being kept as a slave to the French and was always relieved when her master returned.

Winter in the fort proved to be easier in most respects. She was glad to eat the Frenchmen's bread and the familiar salt pork. But she knew the French were responsible for convincing the Indians to fight the colonists. Had the Indian nations not allied with the French, her family would not have been massacred and she would not be a slave. This knowledge made life in the French fort almost unbearable.

Spring finally came and Galasko led their party more than two hundred miles deeper into the western wilderness. They crossed the great Ohio River with little difficulty, but when they came to the Muskegon, the spring rains had swollen the river, making the crossing impossible. When the river's rushing waters finally lowered, they were able to cross safely. On the other side, they came to the Indian village named Moschkingo — the village of Galasko's father, Chief Selingquaw. After over a year and a half of captivity, Galasko declared they were home.

At first glance, Moschkingo appeared similar to Kittanny, with its long houses, barking dogs, women and children working, and the braves standing about, resting from a recent hunt or long journey. As they drew nearer, a surge of life filled the faces of the women, young and old alike. It was as if a face they had feared they would never see again had suddenly appeared. The natives rushed forward to welcome Galasko and his braves. A hollow, empty feeling came over Barbara. Seeing others joyfully welcomed home by loved ones made her long for her own family.

With similar eagerness, but in its own unique way, the tribe also extended a welcome to Marie and Barbara. They gave each of them three strong pats on the back, which was the custom of their tribe. As Barbara went down the line of those gathered, she was glad they seemed eager to accept her. But still the longing for her own home and family left her feeling sick inside.

When she got to the end of the line, a tall warrior, who bore the marks of many battles, stood before her. Barbara's heart beat a little faster. He stood staring down at her as if he recognized her. He then turned down his lower lip, grunted, and walked away. Did she know him? Had she offended him? Stunned, Barbara stood still for a moment, and then everything came back to her. The face, the tall build, the strong, coiled demeanor that seemed ready to strike when angered—it was Galasko's brother,

Hannawoa. She had never understood his behavior, and she had always wondered why he had not traveled with them. Had he continued his raids on the unsuspecting settlers?

"Do not let him scare you," a voice said. Barbara was surprised to find a young man standing next to her. He dressed, talked, and acted like a native, but his soft hazel eyes gave him away. He motioned for Barbara to step out of earshot of the others. "Hannawoa is jealous of his brother. He is the older brother of Galasko and a great warrior, but he is a fierce, bitter man. His father, the chief, favors Galasko's kind ways. Hannawoa will not harm you if you stay out of his way. I know his temperament well. He captured me and another English boy."

Barbara stared in amazement at the young man. He seemed tall and strong for his age, but could not have been older than eleven. His boldness and courage impressed her. "What is your name?" she asked.

"My English name is Owen Gibson, but my master lost a son in battle and has adopted me as his own. My Indian name is Souchy, or Second Son. My friend David's name is Kalasquay." Owen pointed across camp at another boy about his own age.

Just then Marie rushed up. The color had drained from her cheeks, and it was obvious that something was wrong.

"Marie, what is it?" she asked.

"Barbara, I have just overheard the worst news," Marie said. "The chief has promised one of us to an ancient woman who lives in this village. She has lost her husband

and children and lives in want. Galasko says *I* am to go live with her."

"Surely you misunderstood," Barbara said as her thoughts went back to when she and Regina were separated. "I won't let them take you away."

"Barbara, will you talk to Galasko?" Marie asked. "He always listens to you."

It wasn't until later that afternoon that Barbara finally had the opportunity to approach Galasko. He had just left his father and mother's long house and was headed back toward the Muskegon River. Barbara had been watching him throughout the day, and she was surprised to see how much respect and authority Galasko had in the village. As Chief Selingquaw's son, he held both honor and responsibility. This gave her courage as she approached him. She hoped he would find a way to make things right.

Barbara asked and then pleaded with Galasko to let Marie live with her under the same master as they had from the beginning.

Speaking in his native tongue, he firmly yet gently refused. "It is my father's wish. You ask a dangerous thing when you ask me to disobey the chief's command. You cannot live with your friend forever. Someday she will marry and bear many children."

Galasko's statement caught Barbara off guard. She nodded absently and walked away from his presence. She knew many white captives were forced to marry into the tribe, but it had never occurred to her that she and Marie were nearing their marrying age. Barbara assured herself that they had at least a couple of years before that could happen, and then she quickly dismissed the alarming thought.

Chapter 7

INDIAN BRIDE

*B*arbara and Marie's chores gave them little time to visit, but at least they were together during the day. Life in the village settled into a sort of routine with spring planting, and then the many summer activities. Barbara liked basket weaving and making pottery the best, though she had her share of cleaning wild game. Then there was the busy fall harvest and the cold winter days spent skinning and tanning hides and pelts.

It did not take Barbara long to make friends among the young maidens and children of the village. The tribe made it clear that they did not think of her as a white enemy, but as one of their own. From the start, Barbara had noticed one young maiden in particular whose dark brown eyes overflowed with kindness and who always danced with merriment as if she found secret delight in befriending Marie and her. They called her Hylea, The

Light of the Morning Star. Barbara knew they would soon be friends. And they were. The months passed with increasing speed. Summer came and went and came again.

"I cannot believe that our second summer here is coming to an end," Marie said one day as they watched the braves prepare for their late summer Green Corn Festival.

"We have had a good crop this year. The celebrating should go long into the night." Barbara smiled at Hylea, who called out a greeting as they passed her long house. "Yes, the braves will dance and thank their great spirit for the good crops, but I often wonder what spirit they worship." Barbara decided she would ask Galasko that night during the ceremony.

He always gave Barbara special attention. Hylea often teased Barbara and said he was in love with her, but Barbara chose not to believe it. She knew Galasko had admired her courageous spirit but felt sure his feelings did not go beyond respect. Hylea insisted that, if Barbara would only look at herself in the reflection of the waters, she would know she was beautiful.

"Besides," Hylea would say, "all the young braves know Galasko secretly wants to someday marry you. Why else do they treat you with respect? They know not to bother the future wife of the chief's son." Her eyes would sparkle with mischief and a happy laugh would fill the air. "I cannot think of any other maiden who deserves such a strong and brave warrior."

"Hylea, that's enough!" Barbara had insisted. "Galasko

is a good master and is kind to everyone. I have not sensed anything more." After Hylea's comments, Barbara found it more difficult to talk comfortably with Galasko. But after a while, she once again convinced herself that he was uninterested.

The Green Corn Festival began with many games and contests for the children and braves, followed by much celebrating and feasting throughout the village. The women worked long and hard to prepare a great feast of wild venison, fresh vegetables, and Indian pudding. The men prepared a giant fire and dressed up, displaying their brightly beaded belts made of wampum. The women and children ornamented themselves with colorful ribbons they got when they traded for furs with a trapper. Some even wore silver broaches. Barbara knew where most of those had come from, and she had to force herself not to think of it lest she become resentful.

After the feasting, dancing began. The great fire flickered and snapped as the warriors danced to their great spirit. From the darkness where Barbara sat, the shadows doubled the size of the decorated braves. She always held back and chose not to join the customary dances. The cries and shrieks made the hair on the back of her neck stand up. She knew this was their way of thanking their god of the harvest, but the rituals always made her feel uneasy. She wished they could understand that the white man's God was their Creator, not their enemy.

"Why does Susquehanna look so sober?"

Barbara looked up. The firelight, which flickered on

Galasko's face, shone brightly one moment and then left them in complete darkness the next. Barbara could see the concern in his eyes. "Galasko, who is your Creator?" she asked.

Galasko's features softened. "Many moons ago, Sky-Woman was pushed out of the heavens and landed on a deserted island—"

"Who made the island?" she asked.

"The island was created when a muskrat brought a bit of mud from under the great sea and placed it on a turtle shell. The turtle grew and so did the land. It formed a great island with rich soil. Sky-Woman lived on the island for some time. When she returned to the heavens, she gave birth to a daughter. Her daughter, in turn, gave birth to two sons, Great Spirit and Evil Spirit. Great Spirit returned to the turtle shell and created the seas, rivers, mountains, and valleys. Finally, he made man. His brother, Evil Spirit, worked too, only he created anger, strife, warfare, and all kinds of dangerous living creatures. When Great Spirit saw what his brother had done, there was a great battle. Evil Spirit lost and was cast into the netherworld, but his creations stayed behind and lived in the children of earth."

"Galasko, if this is true," Barbara asked, "then who created the Sky-Woman, the sea, the muskrat, and the turtle shell?"

Galasko looked confused, as if he had never considered this question. Barbara surprised even herself by her boldness.

"You say the Great Spirit created the sea and living things, but you also say the muskrat, the mud of the sea, and the turtle shell created earth. The God I worship created all things. He created the heavens, the earth, and everything—"

"White man's God is a great god," Galasko said. "He made Susquehanna more graceful than the deer in the meadow and with the courage of a great mountain lion. For this, he is a good God. But, white man's God not Indians' god." Galasko turned and briskly walked away.

It troubled Barbara that Galasko and his people were so lost. They knew both good and evil existed, but they had no guide other than their own customs to teach them the difference. They had no knowledge of the Savior, who died for their sins. They did not know of his Word, the Bible, to show them how to live free of fear, torment, and guilt. They did not understand his love for them.

Barbara was also troubled by Galasko's compliments. She had seen the look in his eyes when he told her God had made her more graceful than the deer. Barbara rushed into the darkness and made her way through the empty village to her long house. If he were to marry her, she would never be able to escape and never see her family again. She *must* have time to think.

After the Green Corn Festival, Galasko paid more attention to Barbara. His gifts and special treatment made her heart grow more anxious. One day after a hunt, he placed a deer outside the long house. It was the largest kill of the winter hunt, and it made all the maidens in the village smile and talk among themselves. On another day, he brought her new moccasins with beautiful beadwork.

Later that afternoon, Barbara was gathering roots in the woods. Marie noticed her friend's new moccasins. "Oh! Barbara, how lovely." Marie looked down at her own cold, bare feet. "Are they not the warmest and most comfortable shoes you have ever worn?"

Barbara could see Marie did not understand. The old woman Marie lived with was harsh and cruel. All she had noticed was that Barbara was treated better. Marie had not thought of what Galasko's attentions might mean for Barbara.

"Marie, do not envy me." She buried her face in her hands and cried uncontrollably for some time. "The winter is almost over, and I fear I will have to marry Galasko. He *has* been a kind master, but how can I marry the man who had a part in killing my father and brother?"

Marie looked shocked and then horrified all in one instant. "Forgive me, Barbara. I did not understand. All I noticed was how good he has been. I did not realize his intentions were for marriage. Now I see clearly. You cannot … you *must* not marry him." Marie looked deep into her friend's eyes as if to assure Barbara of her utmost support no matter what course they had to take to free her from the intended marriage.

"Not only did he kill our loved ones," Marie said, "but his god is not our God—therefore his ways will never be our ways. Our only choice is escape … and we must not put it off lest we are too late!"

Barbara's heart filled with a sudden burst of hope. "You are right, Marie. That is our only choice."

Then Barbara shuddered as she remembered the terrible fate of Lydia when she had tried to escape. "You know if we get caught, we will be tortured and burned at the stake." Barbara paused, thought deeply, and then went on with calm resolve. "Even if the braves do not catch us, there is a very slim chance we would survive in the vast wilderness. That is why I do not want you to risk it for my sake."

Marie grabbed Barbara's hand and immediately tried to protest, but it was no use. "No, I have thought this through," Barbara insisted. "I could never marry Galasko if I knew I had even the slightest chance of escape. But I would never ask you, my dear friend, to risk your life for my sake." As Barbara's resolve grew, so did her courage. "No! You stay here, and if I make it safely, I will not rest until the English win the war and you and all the captives are freed!"

Chapter 8

HANNAWOA

The silvery moon began its ascent into the night sky. The light illuminated the Indian village just enough to make out the forms of the long houses that stood frozen in the early spring frost. Barbara's heart beat so hard that her temples throbbed. She cast many anxious glances through the entrance of her hut. Barbara's mind raced as the lazy moon rose at an agonizingly slow pace. Suddenly, something cold nudged her shoulder. Barbara froze as it sniffed its way up her neck to her face.

The dogs! She had forgotten about them. Barbara reached out to assure the animal of her friendship. At least sixteen dogs were in their village. How could she sneak out of camp without alerting them? Unable to think of any way to secure her escape, Barbara fervently prayed that God would quiet the animals, just as he had shut the lions' mouths in the Book of Daniel.

Barbara thought about the last night she was at home with her family. Her father had read Scripture from their big family Bible. She remembered the verse her family had recited together, and she whispered, " ... the Lord thy God led thee these forty years in the wilderness, to humble thee, and to prove thee, to know what was in thine heart, whether thou wouldest keep his commandments or no." She could almost hear her father's voice as he had admonished each of them to always keep their hearts true to their faith, even in the most difficult trial.

"He will never leave you," Papa had said. Then her family had sung the hymn they all loved so well.

She could almost hear her mother's gentle voice and see Regina's smiling face as they had sung that night. Suddenly, the same peace and tranquility that had filled her heart then flooded her soul. At this moment, when she was trying to attempt the impossible, she felt the same divine security. It was as if the Lord was assuring her that, though she felt alone in this vast wilderness, he would never forsake her. No matter what happened, she would not be alone.

She waited as the moon continued its maddeningly slow ascent. As Barbara thought of Regina, her heart ached. She yearned to see her sister's animated face and her twinkling blue eyes. But most of all, Barbara longed to know if Regina still held on to the song in her heart.

Then her thoughts moved on to Galasko and the last day she had seen him. Shortly after Chief Selingquaw had announced their intended marriage, the tribe received word that Fort Duquesne had fallen to the English and was now Fort Pitt. Though this wonderful news had given hope to Marie and Barbara, the Indian warriors were greatly disturbed with the success of their enemies. They immediately answered the summons of the French and set out to recapture the lost ground.

Just before they left, Galasko turned to Barbara. Calling her Susquehanna, he had assured her he would return with the melting of the snow, and they would be married beneath the blossoms of spring. He told her the stars in the heavens would be like a field of wildflowers, reminding her of his ever-constant affection.

Barbara shivered at the gloomy prospect.

The warriors departed with such resolve that they had left only two braves behind to guard the women and children. One of the braves was the merciless Hannawoa. The sight of him every day and the thought of what he might do if she failed in her attempt to escape frightened Barbara. But she knew the time had come. If she were ever to see her mother again and find her sister, she must leave now.

Marie had convinced Barbara to allow her and the two English boys to escape with her.

"There is strength in numbers," Marie urged, "and with the boys, though they are but twelve and thirteen, the chances of surviving are greatly increased." It did not take Barbara long to realize Marie was right. Soon they had not only completed their well-devised plans, but also their preparations for the long journey. When the snows began to melt, they had known the day drew near.

The evening before, Barbara had pretended to be sick so she would be placed in an isolated hut—the same hut she was now so eager to leave. The plan had worked, and she must leave shortly to meet the others on the banks of the Muskegon River.

Seeing that the moon had reached its zenith, Barbara stuck her head out into the night air to get a clear view of her solitary position in the midst of the village.

"There," she thought to herself, "the moon is at its peak and the others will be waiting for me at the river." Once more she asked God to keep the watchdogs from barking and grabbed a tomahawk, a knife, and a little store of salvaged provisions wrapped in some deer hide. Shivering, she slipped into the darkness of the night.

Ever so quietly, Barbara crept through the village. It seemed like an eternity before she neared the outskirts. Out of the corner of her eye, she caught a movement. She froze and then turned to look. To the side of a nearby long house she saw the shadow of a human figure. It was coming her way. She hoped it was Marie or one of the boys. Unsure, she decided to hide behind a woodpile and wait—just to be safe.

Barbara tried to still her fast breathing. She knew the slightest sound might forfeit her life. The shadow grew considerably before the form broke around the corner. Barbara's heart was gripped by fear, sending a chilling shiver up her spine. It was Hannawoa!

He was scouting the camp just to be sure all was in order. He always seemed to sense if anything was out of the ordinary. Afraid to move, Barbara stayed hidden where she was. Finally, the stoic brave continued his search in a different part of the village.

"That was too close," she whispered as she let out a sigh of relief. She hoped the others had managed to sneak out of camp without being caught. Barbara's heart hammered as she crossed the last bit of open ground. She felt as if the glistening moon was focusing all of its soft beams on her, and for a painfully long moment she was certain Hannawoa would come back and see her. Fighting the urge to look back across the clearing, she pressed on into the safety of the woods. Soon the shadows of the forest blended with her own until she was completely enveloped in the thick veil of the slumbering forest. But Barbara raced on at full speed, anxious to see if the others had made it safely to their chosen meeting place.

Chapter 9

THE FLIGHT

*B*arbara?" A quiet whisper filtered its way through the thick vines and brush that covered the banks of the Muskegon River.

Barbara recognized Marie's voice. "Yes," she replied softly, knowing her words could echo across the wide river before them. It looked placid in the reflection of the moonlight, but the vast expanse of water could turn into their greatest enemy if not approached with care.

She knelt down on her hands and knees and felt her way through the brush. The thick undergrowth shut out most of the moonlight, and it took a moment for Barbara's eyes to adjust to the darkness. Finally, she made out a black form, peering from behind a tree trunk.

"Right here, Barbara." Marie reached out her hand and pulled Barbara into her hiding place.

"I just saw Hannawoa searching the village." Barbara

87

tightened her grip on Marie's hand. "Where are the boys? Are they out of the village?"

"They are searching for a log we can use to build a raft."

It was then that Barbara noticed the musket Marie clasped tightly. "How did you manage to get that?" she asked.

"It's Owen's hunting musket," Marie said. "He thought I might need it while I waited here for you."

Barbara nodded gravely. "It is a good thing his Indian master did not realize his desire to escape, or he would never have treated Owen as his adopted son and given him this hunting musket to mark his passage into manhood."

Barbara could feel Marie shivering.

"I am so frightened," Marie said.

"Everything is going to be all right." Barbara tried to reassure her friend. "God is with us."

"I know, but I cannot forget what happened to Lydia."

The sight of the young English woman being burned at the stake blazed in Barbara's mind too. She refused to dwell on it.

"That will not happen to us. Galasko would never allow it."

"But Hannawoa is in charge. He is so cruel. What if he did something before Galasko returns?"

Barbara stroked Marie's hair. "Hush. Do not think of it. We would never attempt this escape if we did not know God is with us. We will make it. I know we will."

Marie's shivering eased, but Barbara wondered what the future held. Would they make it across the river? And if they did make it, what would happen then? How could they survive? *Dear God, help me be strong. Help me to trust you,* she silently prayed.

Just then, Owen, the oldest of the boys, emerged from the darkness. "Come quickly, we found a raft a short way down the river," he said in a voice that could have easily been heard if someone were listening.

"Shhh," whispered Barbara, "you might be heard."

"Hurry, David is waiting," he urged more quietly.

Owen motioned for the musket and Marie gladly allowed him to take charge of it. They followed Owen as he worked his way down to the water's edge. After trudging through the thick mud of the riverbank, they found David waiting for them in a small inlet. The raft was crude, but it would hold the four of them and their meager supplies.

A thought suddenly struck Barbara. She pointed at their muddy footprints. "Hannawoa will be able to track us. When we reach the other side of the river, we must remember to walk backward over the soft earth so our trail looks like it is going back across the river toward the west." Galasko had shown her how to disguise her tracks so the British colonials could not find her. Now she was grateful.

Clouds moved across the face of the moon, darkening the night. The four of them climbed aboard. Owen handed Barbara his musket before he launched the raft into the steady current. Barbara looked over her shoulder as the shoreline disappeared in the darkness. A cold gust of wind caught her hair and whipped it around her cheeks.

The river was swollen due to the melting winter snows and the current was strong. David and Owen had to use all their strength to fight its motion as it swirled and churned around their makeshift birch oars.

The boys' arms grew heavy with fatigue. Barbara could not only see their faltering strength but also hear it in their groans. Marie whimpered with fear. Barbara's heart pounded with adrenaline and she could feel the blood surging through her veins. She breathed deeply. *I must be strong.* With one hand, she gripped Owen's musket. With her other hand, Barbara took Marie's hand. The words of a German hymn she sung as a child came to mind.

"Dear God, bring us safely across the river!" She softly prayed the words aloud, changing them to fit the present danger. "My soul trembles at the hardship before us. The river is wide and the wilderness wider still. Yet, dear Lord, I would risk cold and hunger to flee from the ways of those who do not worship you. Help us, great God, and stretch out your mighty hand."

Barbara's heart quieted and she felt a peaceful assurance. "I will always trust in you," she continued, "for I know that you are near. You will never leave—"

Owen's desperate cry broke her heartfelt prayer.

"There's the bank! Paddle harder or we will miss the cove!" David and Owen strained in the effort to turn their raft in the direction he had pointed. In the near distance, they could hear the raging rapids where the river forked. If they did not make the shore now, they would be dashed to pieces on the rocks.

Barbara held her breath and grasped Marie's hand even tighter.

"Steady now!" Owen shouted over the tumultuous waters that twisted and surged around them. "Row hard left!" David groaned as he put all of his strength into fighting the current. Then, just as quickly as the rapids had come upon them, they glided safely into the sheltering harbor of the little cove. They were safe.

After quickly jumping into the shallow waters, they shoved their little vessel back into the restless current. Barbara watched the abandoned raft skip and dance in the moonlight as the fierce waters carried it downriver. Then she could hear it being torn to pieces against the boulders.

"Let's go," whispered Barbara. She showed Marie how to walk backward so it looked as if they were going in the opposite direction. "We must flee quickly! Hannawoa was searching the village when I left. He must have already sensed that something is different. Our head start ends with the morning light. If — if it hasn't already."

Chapter 10

PAIN AND HUNGER

*S*oon they were on high, firm ground. The moon had already begun to set and they knew they had just a few hours until sunrise.

They climbed a steep, wooded incline that overlooked the river. Then they stumbled their way in the darkness through the tangled undergrowth. Still they ran on.

The thick vines and low branches of the forest ripped at Barbara until she could feel the sting of fresh cuts and scratches and blood trickling down her face and arms. Her sides ached with fatigue, and she longed to slow her pace. But fear of Hannawoa urged her to continue.

Whenever one of them stumbled with weariness or fell faint with exhaustion, the others were right there encouraging them to not give up. Each time, the hope of freedom, mixed with the fear of capture, stirred their hearts until they once again burned with the desire to run on.

They continued their desperate flight through the night and into late morning. Just before the sun reached noon, the weary party stumbled upon a sunlit meadow. The sun had melted away the ice on a small stream that ran through it. Exhausted and thirsty, they dropped down on a flat stone that fringed the stream and hurriedly drank from the cool fresh waters. Then, unraveling the leather straps from her deer hide satchel, Barbara divided her provisions of dried berries and meat.

Marie took a deep breath. "We are safe," she sighed.

But Barbara knew it was far too early to tell. Even if Hannawoa did not catch them, it would be a miracle if they survived the journey through the mountainous forests. The nearest English outpost was over two hundred miles through the wilderness, and they were about to eat all the provisions they had. After that, their survival depended on the roots they could find and the wild game they could hunt.

"I have enough powder and lead to get four good shots from my musket," Owen said as if he had read her mind. "That ought to bring food enough to last a fortnight."

"This may be true," said David, "but we can't shoot any game for some time." These were the first words Barbara had heard David speak all morning. He squinted and nodded his head toward the sun. "Hannawoa is no doubt on our trail by now. We must keep going."

Without another word, Barbara tightened the waistband of her buckskin dress, secured her tomahawk, and gathered what was left of their rations. Owen swung his powder horn back around his neck and picked up his musket. David led the way as they plunged back into the shadows of the forest. They ran with renewed strength and fear.

It wasn't until after the full moon had risen that night that they looked back. They found shelter near the top of a ridge. Here they had the advantage of scanning the valley to the west—to watch for Hannawoa.

Barbara insisted that she keep watch for the first shift. "My mind will not rest. It would be a waste for me to lie awake while someone else lost sleep."

It didn't take the others long to agree. Soon they fell into a much-needed sleep.

Barbara perched on the top of the ridge and vigilantly searched the shadows that bound the tree-lined valley below. At first, all her senses were alive, and each tree that creaked or branch that swayed in the slight spring breeze alerted her. Barbara looked at the shimmering stars above and wondered what the next days would bring.

She thought of Regina and wondered if she were in a village nearby, watching the same starlit canopy above. Looking back at the tranquil valley, she remembered how she and Regina used to chase fireflies together at home. One time they were so thick that they looked like little stars dancing and flashing about. The pleasant memory so soothed Barbara's mind that, before long, the sights and sounds of the night blended together in harmony, and she fell into a deep sleep.

Barbara awoke with a start. It was early morning.

"Wake up, wake up!" She turned and shook Marie, who slept nearby. "We have lost at least an hour of daylight, and Hannawoa will surely be that much closer."

Owen rubbed his eyes, stared blankly for a moment, and then said, "Oh no! How did I oversleep?"

Within minutes they were rushing down the ridge with fresh determination. The few hours of sleep had provided them with new energy, but by afternoon, Barbara's whole body felt weak. Each step seemed to drain her strength until finally she trembled from hunger and fatigue. She looked at Marie, who stumbled behind her. David tried to help her, but he too was exhausted and unstable.

Barbara looked up the trail at Owen and said, "We must slow our pace to a walk until we find food; otherwise I fear we will never make it."

Owen nodded as he wiped beads of sweat from his brow. "I think you are right, but we must be careful to hide our trail whenever we can. I hear a stream ahead. We will walk in it for a while to hide our tracks."

Near evening they felt they had distanced themselves enough from the Indians to shoot at some game. As they watched Owen disappear over a hill, David assured Barbara that his friend was a brave hunter.

An hour later Barbara and Marie stared in disbelief as Owen returned from his hunt. His leg was bloodied and he was limping badly. They forgot all about their gnawing hunger pains and quickly saw to his gushing wound. Marie did her best to clean the gashes, picking out small pieces of leaves and dirt, while Barbara cut hide with the

1 Papa teaching Barbara how to defend herself.
2 Hannawoa getting ready to take back their tribal lands.
3 Galasko, youngest son of Chief Selingquaw.
4 Galasko and Hannawoa enter cabin and attack.

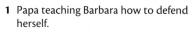

1 Galasko and Hannawoa
capture Barbara and
Regina.

2 Barbara makes Regina
promise never to lose
the song in her heart.

3 Regina and Barbara are
separated by two tribes.

4 Barbara hides two young boys during their escape from Kittanning Village.
5 Young Barbara (played by Natalie Racoosin) grinding corn at Kittanning Village.
6 Colonel Armstrong rehearses a fight scene before filming.
7 The captives enter Fort du Quesne.

1

2

1 Artificial snow is applied in preparation for a shot at Fort du Quesne.
2 Galasko takes aim at a buffalo.
3 The crew prepares for Barbara burning at the stake.

3

4 Fort due Quesne set located at Fort Loudoun.
5 Barbara in Moschkingo Village with Hylea and Hylea's mother.
6 Barbara is indoctrinated into the tribe as her hair and skin are dyed with walnut juice.
7 The captives move upstream seeking their freedom.

1 The captives plan for freedom.
2 Under attack!
3 Hannawoa tracking the runaways.
4 The captives narrowly escape.

5 Behind-the-scenes at Bridal Veil Falls.
6 The captives escape through the waterfall at Bridal Veil Falls.
7 Barbara (Susquehanna) emerges from the Ohio River on her escape.

1. From left to right: Clay Walker (Fritz), Ray Bengston (Director), Joanie Stewart (Momma), Brett Harris (Owen), Kelly Greyson (Barbara), Victoria Emmons (Marie).

2. The Red Coats investigate the captives dressed in their native garb.

3. The Leininger family thanks God for his blessings at Christmas dinner.

tool she carried to cut their food into strips. David bandaged the wound the best he could.

Owen looked pale, but he maintained his composure as he recounted his story. "I hit the bear on my first shot, and he went right down. I was sure it was a solid hit and rushed it with my tomahawk." Owen closed his eyes in pain and gritted his teeth, as Barbara tightened her makeshift tourniquet around the open wound. "The next thing I knew, the bear lunged toward me with so much strength that I wondered if my shot had even penetrated his thick coat. When I tried to dodge him, I wasn't quick enough, and he caught my leg with his jaws. I struck him with my tomahawk and tried to pull my leg away, but that only made him angrier. I thought for sure he would eat me alive, but just like that, he released my leg, and I ran off. I guess it took awhile for my first shot to take effect."

"Then what happened?" David asked. "You knew he was wounded. Did you shoot him again?"

Owen looked surprised at his friend's sudden outburst, but then he hung his head. "No, he was too far away by the time I got my musket loaded again. I am sorry. I know you all were counting on me. You could follow his blood trail, but I'm afraid it would do no good. He's probably hiding out in a cave by now."

After that their progress slowed considerably. Owen's injury was the main hindrance, but they were also tired and hungry. Finally, on the third day, Owen fired a successful shot at a deer. Barbara and Marie helped him clean it while David built a fire with his flint and steel.

Barbara's hand trembled from hunger as she stuck a long pointed stick through her piece of meat and roasted it over the fire. Marie talked constantly and seemed to be herself for the first time since leaving the village. Barbara could tell that they all held greater hope than they had since their escape.

When Barbara could not eat any more, she helped the boys cut the extra venison into strips and hang them near the fire to dry overnight. Then, with a sense of satisfaction, she sat close to the warmth of the campfire and watched the glow of the embers.

The distant cry of an owl caught her attention. No doubt it was perched high in one of the tall maple or birch trees that grew in the surrounding forest. Suddenly, Barbara felt small compared to the untouched wilderness. She remembered when she had last traveled through it with Galasko. She thought it would never end and could not believe human beings lived so far from civilization. When she was with Galasko, though, she was never worried that they would get lost or be harmed by wild animals. He was always there and seemed to know how to read the signs of the forest, better than a white man could read a well-drawn map.

Barbara looked back at the fire. They did not have Galasko, but God was with them and he had already been so good to them. She thought through the events of the last few days. Hannawoa had not caught her when she sneaked out of the village. They safely crossed the river. Owen could have been killed by that bear, but escaped with only a leg wound. And now, after three days in the dense wilderness, she was sitting by a warm fire with a full stomach.

Barbara laid her head on a soft bed of spruce boughs she had gathered. She knew they still had hundreds of miles to travel, but the Lord had already provided all their needs. He would continue to be with them.

The next morning they wrapped up the mostly dried meat and set out toward the rising sun. They knew their only hope of ever finding their families was to push eastward. Mile after mile they pressed on through the thick forest, making considerable headway over the next two days. They only stopped to drink or to check the angle of the sun on the tall maple and pine trees that towered above them. When the light faded in the evening, they would study the trunks. Knowing that moss grew heaviest on the north side of the tree, they could tell which way was east.

By the evening of the fifth day, the party had reached the Ohio River. It was swollen and stretched out before them for at least a half-mile. Barbara was eager to cross it, but first, they had to find a way. After much discussion, they decided their only choice was to build another raft.

They found a camp with a small shelter and even some dry firewood. The Indians had evidently used it while traveling east for fur trade.

"Look at this," Marie said, pointing to a tree. The markings on it showed they still had over one hundred and fifty miles to journey before they reached Fort Pitt.

Barbara felt relieved to know they were on the right trail, but somewhat discouraged by the distance yet to be traveled. Her muscles were sore and she felt exhausted. All she wanted to do was rest, but there was still much to do.

"If we can just make it to the other side," she said, "then we can rest." She glanced uneasily over her shoulder. Even though the sight of the Ohio River meant they had put over one hundred miles between themselves and the Indian village, Barbara knew it would be foolish to underestimate Hannawoa's tracking abilities. Worse, they were now camped on what looked like a main Indian trail.

Owen placed his hand on Barbara's shoulder. "Don't worry. David and I will build the raft tonight while you and Marie get some rest. We will cross first thing in the morning."

Barbara was grateful to Owen. She had tried to hide her fear, but he had somehow sensed it. "You are right; I know God will provide. It is easy to lose perspective when you are tired—I was just a little discouraged, that is all," she said, trying to smile. "I will get a fire going so you can get started."

Soon the fire was blazing, and Barbara unpacked their dried venison. Owen and David gathered good-sized pieces of driftwood for the raft, and Marie found enough pliable undergrowth and tender vines to weave into a rope. After a quick meal, the boys insisted the girls sleep while they worked.

"We will work all night if we have to, but the raft will be ready in the morning," David assured them.

Barbara smiled her thanks and turned toward the shelter. For once, she did not insist on staying up to help.

Chapter 11

THE DANGEROUS CROSSING

Barbara stood on the west shore of the Ohio River and searched the opposite bank. The bright morning sun reflected off the water and it nearly blinded her.

"It is not the largest or the sturdiest raft I have ever seen, but it will have to do," Owen said, standing over his creation.

"If we keep still, I think we can make it across," David said with his usual cautious tone and an expression of concern. "Crossing a swollen river on a makeshift raft is not the safest. We must be careful."

Barbara did not care about the danger. The farther she was from Hannawoa, the better. She would risk anything just to get to the other side of the Ohio.

After climbing onto the raft, they launched it into the water. Using long, thin poles, Owen and David pushed it away from shore. The steady current carried them into the middle of the river. They were halfway across when the current picked up and began to sweep them along at an alarming rate. Large pieces of driftwood and debris banged against their small raft, making it seem even smaller. It was all they could do to stay upright.

Barbara took a deep breath and focused on the far shore, hoping to ease the growing tension she felt. *Dear God!* she prayed silently. Her knuckles whitened from her desperate grip on the raft.

"Look behind you!" David shouted. A large log headed right toward Barbara's side of the raft.

"Barbara! Watch out!" he yelled. But it was too late. The log hit the corner of the raft, upsetting her balance. She fell backward, grabbing frantically for something firm, but the impact knocked her into the surging river.

The shock of the freezing cold water stunned Barbara. She tried to breathe but instead gulped in a mouthful of cold, murky water. The churning current engulfed her. She flailed her arms and gasped for air.

"Dear God!" she cried. "Help me find the raft!" The water's pull was strong and Barbara did not know how to swim. She could feel herself being swept away. The turbulent suction of the rapids pulled her down into the darkness. Her heart surged with adrenaline. She felt dizzy and her lungs ached.

Suddenly, Barbara felt her hair catch in something that stopped her plunge and pulled her against the current. Slowly, she was being dragged toward the light above. Barbara broke through the water's surface. She gasped for air and then looked into Owen's face. Despite the pain of his wound, he had jumped in the raging river and risked his life to rescue her.

Owen placed his arm securely under her shoulder and swam toward the raft, which was about twenty yards from where they had surfaced.

As David pulled Barbara out of danger, Marie's desperate screams tore through the air. With his last ounce of strength, Owen climbed onto the raft after Barbara and collapsed, panting for air.

David returned to his post at the front of the raft and continued paddling. It took several minutes before Owen had the strength to join him. In the meantime, Marie sobbed uncontrollably. Barbara coughed and sputtered, totally spent from the incident. Marie wrapped her arms around Barbara's cold, shivering form and further soaked her already-wet shoulder with tears.

Barbara sat in complete shock for a moment, recalling the rapid events that had just taken place. Then she looked at Marie. Finding her reaction a bit dramatic and somehow a little funny, Barbara laughed through her chattering teeth.

"Marie, do I appear dead that you would cry so?" Barbara's smile was a bit wobbly, but she tried hard to console her distraught friend. "Do try to save your tears and help me warm myself. I am numb with cold and fear I might freeze."

Marie immediately stopped her wailing. "Barbara! Your lips are blue!" she exclaimed. "We must get to the other side and start a fire!"

David took off his shirt. "Marie, wrap this around Barbara. It is not much, but it is all I have. We must get her warm." Barbara listened through a foggy mist. She wanted to sleep; she was so cold that she was shivering, but now she felt warm.

"Don't let her sleep." Owen looked at Barbara with deep concern. "Rub her hands, feet, anything. We will be on the other side soon."

They managed to make the opposite bank of the river without any further mishaps. By now Barbara shivered uncontrollably, but she kept insisting that she felt warm and was just fine. Owen ordered everyone to gather some dry wood and leaves, and before long they had a small pile ready to light.

"No!" cried Owen, patting his pockets. "My flint and steel are gone!" He desperately searched the pockets of his buckskins, deep concern written in every crease of his brow. "They must have washed away in the river."

Barbara put her hand to her head and ran her fingers across her forehead and through her wet hair. She kept trying to tell herself she felt fine, but she knew something was terribly wrong. Shivers tingled through her whole body. She closed her eyes and began to pray. Barbara knew they *must* find the flint and steel. How could they survive in the wilderness without means of starting a fire?

Owen and David eagerly searched the raft and through all their belongings. They retraced all of their steps. Nothing.

"I must have lost them when I dove into the water," said Owen, finally sitting down beside Barbara.

"Now what are we going to do?" cried Marie with a fresh flow of tears. "We will die out here without a fire."

Owen looked pale and Barbara could tell they were all thinking the same thing. He glanced at Barbara and jumped up. "The first thing we need to do is keep you moving." Owen took Barbara's hand and helped her to her feet. "Marie, walk with Barbara, while I think of what to do."

"Look." David pointed at the horizon. Low, thick clouds gathered. So far they had not needed to deal with rain or snow, but now it looked like they would soon be facing this new challenge.

Owen gazed back across the river, despair written on his face. Barbara knew what he was thinking. One hundred and fifty miles of snow-covered mountains and valley lay ahead. They must press on without his flint and steel, with no way of starting a fire, and only two bullets left. He knew their survival was entirely up to Providence.

Chapter 12

FRIEND OR FOE

Fort Pitt was rebuilt on the same strategic peninsula where Fort Duquesne had once stood. From
an outsider's view the only difference was the British flag
flying overhead. Early in the evening of March 21, 1759, a
lone sentinel stood guard along the western wall of Fort Pitt.
The snows had nearly melted, and fresh spring colors dotted
the banks of the Allegheny and Monongahela Rivers as the
dogwood trees budded with new life.

The young man's eyes caught a glimpse of movement
in the reeds on the riverbank below. He gripped his musket a bit tighter, fearing it was an Indian. It made its way
down toward the river, and then came into full view. He
laughed. It was only a beaver struggling to pull a felled
sapling down the bank. With a shake of his head and
a slight smile, the sentinel looked toward the western
horizon.

The clouds had hidden the setting sun. But, refusing to be extinguished, it now poured forth all its beauty, sending hues of purple and pink into the background and gracing the edge of each cloud with a silver lining. The scene was so captivating that the sentinel could not help but gaze at the sky as he pondered the events of the day.

After a few moments he dropped his gaze and slowly surveyed the far western bank of the Monongahela River. The river was at least three hundred yards wide, and its waters and banks were slowly blending together into a dark hue of gray.

He heard a far-off cry. At first he thought it was a wolf or a loon, but no—there it was again. This time he could detect the direction it came from. He combed the western bank of the river, looking for the source. There on the opposite bank stood four figures. The sentinel rushed to report his sighting.

Barbara and the others stood cold, half-starved, and weary from their long, perilous journey. It had been eleven days since their dangerous Ohio River crossing. Barbara remembered how she had thought they would never make it after Owen lost his flint and steel. She had been so cold. Then David had thought to dry-fire Owen's musket with black powder and wadding. They knew each grain of gunpowder was precious, but there was no other choice. They had to try.

David had peeled the driest and smallest pieces of birch bark off the tree trunks and laid them in the shelter of a large spruce grove away from the wind. Sleet began to fall, biting into their already-freezing hands and faces. He added the gunpowder and fired his gun into the small pile of kindling. The sparks from the flintlock sputtered to the ground and the bits of wood caught fire. He nursed the small flame, and soon they had a blazing fire to warm themselves. The sheltering branches of the spruce trees shielded them from the worst of the sleet that was now falling in heavy sheets. Kneeling down, they all thanked God that he had once again spared their lives.

Barbara thought of each event that had followed. They had found a well-used Indian footpath leading eastward, but the way before them was miraculously void of people; they never encountered a single soul. They had traveled through mountain ranges and swamps and broken through what seemed to be an impenetrable forest. Their last two musket shots had supplied just enough game to give them the nourishment they needed. And now, just when they were out of all resources, he had led them to the fort. Barbara knew only the hand of God could have brought them to this place — a refuge bordered on all sides by miles of vast wilderness.

When they had first crested the ridge above the river and sighted the fort nestled between the two rivers, Barbara had gripped Marie's hand and stared in disbelief. She had dreamed of such a moment for so long that the reality refused to sink in. Then, with tears of joy streaming down her face, she hugged her friend. They had made it!

With renewed energy, the boys had rushed down the ridge first. Barbara had helped Marie, who was weak from the journey, down to the riverbank. They all waved and yelled, "Hello, hello. Is anyone there?"

But the darkening walls of the fort stood silent, and, except for a thin line of smoke from a fire somewhere within its walls, the place looked deserted.

The boys continued to call, while the girls waved their arms. Still there was no response.

Meanwhile, within the fort, the sentinel had reported to Colonel Mercer that he had spotted four young Indians on the opposite bank—two boys, not yet old enough to be considered warriors, and two young maidens.

"They are hailing the fort, sir. The youngsters appear to be in distress," said the tenderhearted sentinel. "Shall I send a boat to fetch them?"

The colonel listened intently to the description of the children, but his brow furrowed in deep concern at the suggestion of sending a boat across the river. "The children will have to wait until morning." After pondering the matter for a few moments, Colonel Mercer said slowly and deliberately, "They may be children, but they are Indians, and I will remind you that we are in the middle of a war." The colonel cleared his throat. "How are we to know these Indians are our allies? This could be a trick to draw us away from the fort and then ambush us. No, with the rapid approach of nightfall, it is best to wait until the morning light."

Just then a second soldier entered and saluted the colonel. "Sir, I wish to add my own personal observations, if I may. The children on the opposite bank are indeed dressed as Indians. I am sure, however, that they are not speaking an Indian dialect. When listening to their cries for help, they sound very English. This brings me to the conclusion—"

Colonel Mercer stood, and with a gleam of hope in his eyes, he said, "Do you suppose they are white captives? If so, it is not safe to leave them unprotected overnight. Heaven only knows, there might be Indians trailing them, or they could be recaptured by a different marauding tribe."

Colonel Mercer immediately arranged for a group of men to proceed halfway across the river to investigate further.

"Use discretion, men. Do not risk your lives by falling for a sly trick," he warned as the convoy left the fort.

Owen pointed to the middle of the river. A small boat approached. The sentinel, who was aboard the boat, called out, "Who goes there? Are you a friend or foe?"

Barbara looked at Marie. How could they even ask such a question? Then she realized the black walnut juice the Indian women had used to dye their skin and hair had not yet worn off.

"Marie, look at us—look at what we are wearing. They think we are Indians."

At that, Owen called out to assure them they were Indian captives who had come in peace. He used the clearest English accent he could muster, but it had been a long time since he had heard an Englishman speak. Despite his best efforts, his words still bore a slight Indian accent.

"How can you prove this?" was the cautious reply from the boat. Then they heard the officer aboard the boat suggest they wait until morning for further investigations. The thought of being forsaken after coming so close to the end of their journey was more than Barbara could bear.

Marie, though shivering, also cried out in English, "We *do* come in peace. We are white Indian captives who have escaped. Please, oh please, help us." Marie's voice broke into a sob as she tried to continue. "We … we are very hungry and … and …" Marie's words drifted into the wind, and she fell sobbing into Barbara's arms.

Realizing that her friend's words seemed to be having some effect, Barbara hurriedly picked up where she had left off. Only, in her excitement, she spoke her native German tongue instead of English.

"We have lost our flint and steel and our powder horn is empty. We have no means of starting a fire. Please allow us to enter the fort tonight. We are out of lead shot and have no way to protect ourselves from—"

"Barbara!" Owen interrupted with alarm. "You are speaking in German; they cannot understand a—"

A cry came from the boat. "Men! Row to shore. I have yet to meet an Indian who speaks German so perfectly." The five men in the boat cheered and plunged their paddles deep into the water, defying the current and sending the vessel shooting across the remainder of the river. Soon the tip of the boat hit the bank and shouts of joy erupted from both parties as they grasped each other's hands in a warm greeting. A sob caught in Barbara's throat — at last she was free.

After they were safely inside the walls of the fort, and the great doors had closed behind them, Barbara looked around her in amazement. For the first time since that fateful massacre three and a half years earlier, she felt secure. Owen stood silently next to her, and when she looked at his face to share the joy in her heart, she was sure that, there in the last light of the evening, she could see a lone tear trickle down his young face. Barbara looked at David and could see that he too had shed some tears. Her throat tightened as she reflected on the great trials they had been through and the weight of responsibility these young men had borne. Then Barbara looked at Marie, whose constant companionship had been so key to her own survival.

"I am so glad I did not try to escape on my own," she whispered to her friend, who had shared so many of her burdens. Unashamed tears ran down her face. "I am eternally grateful to the Lord for his protection and provision. Now I am free to find my family and my Regina."

Chapter 13

ALMOST HOME!

After several days of warm clothes, soft bedding, and the most delicious food, Barbara, Marie, and the boys were told by Colonel Mercer that they would be given an escort east. He had already sent a courier to notify any surviving relatives of the captives' return. The colonel had also kindly said that one of his frontier militia escorts would accompany them all the way to the capital city of Philadelphia if he had to.

The full reality of freedom did not sink in for Barbara until one month later when the wagon she and Marie were riding in bumped its way down the rutted streets of Philadelphia. Storm clouds gathered overhead, but to Barbara, the day could not have been brighter.

"I will never forget this moment!" Barbara exclaimed. She breathed deeply of the fresh spring breeze and gazed in wonderment at the buildings and houses that lined the streets. Barbara turned to the young militia escort who drove the wagon. "I had forgotten what it is like to be in a city." She looked up at a large structure before her. "It seems so strange yet wondrous to see such grand buildings."

The young escort smiled. "Over there's where the legislature meets. Colonel Mercer gave me orders to bring you to his friend. Says his friend works for the governor of Pennsylvania, and that he'd provide your food and lodgin' 'til your kinfolks come."

"Can we go inside the building?" Marie asked.

"I reckon you will," replied the escort, "but first we're headed to the liv'ry stables. You two can get rid of some of that dust you've collected on the trail while I feed and water the horses."

Barbara nodded, but hardly heard a word the young man said. She was far too caught up in observing the sights and sounds of civilization. The fine-looking carriages with well-groomed horses and fashionably dressed men and women were especially interesting. She was fascinated by the fancy layered dresses with lace trimming the women were wearing. Everyone smiled as they passed.

Barbara remembered being in Philadelphia during the winter months as a young girl. But now, with the freshness of spring mixed with the joy of being surrounded by friendly faces, the city was even more delightful and remarkable.

Marie was so excited that she had not stopped talking since they had entered the city. Barbara wondered how her friend could think of so much to chatter about.

"Just think, Barbara, if we were still with the Indians, you would be married to Galasko by now." Marie laughed slightly and then grew solemn.

Barbara thought of Regina. Where was she right now? Was she safely home with their mother? If not, was her master kind like Galasko? Were the people in her village strong and healthy, or did they suffer hunger and sickness through the winter months?

She thought back to when she had arrived at the village of Kittanny. The corn crop had been bad that year, and she could see the effects of suffering in the thin, drawn faces that had greeted her. What a contrast to the healthy, amiable people who walked along the streets of Philadelphia and bustled past the shop windows. She remembered the feeling of constant cold and hunger. She and the rest of the tribe were forced to overlook their own discomforts and work tirelessly so they could survive. But here, in the city, Barbara could not imagine anyone starving.

Barbara sighed, knowing she would never be completely free until she knew Regina was also free.

Back at Fort Pitt, she had pleaded with Colonel Mercer to send a convoy of soldiers into the wilderness to search for Regina and the other captives Barbara had met throughout her years of captivity. He was sympathetic and seemed understanding, but nevertheless he explained to her the impossibilities of such a mission.

"You see," the colonel said with deep concern in his eyes, "more than just a handful of our children have experienced your sister's plight. There are hundreds." The colonel had sighed. "We must all pray that we will see the end of this cruel war soon."

Marie grabbed her arm, bringing her thoughts back to the streets of Philadelphia. "Oh, Barbara, look!" Marie pointed at a shop window. In it, a beautiful blue dress trimmed in delicate lace was displayed. "Is that not the loveliest thing you have ever seen?" Marie's voice trailed off.

Barbara smiled, amused at her friend's dramatic expression as Marie studied each tuck and pleat.

"You would look like a princess in it," Marie said.

Barbara laughed with delight at the thought of being dressed in such an elegant fashion. Soon their wagon rolled on and the shop and its dress were hidden from their sight. But Marie still prattled on. "I do hope I can get some new clothes. I just know I will hear from my relatives soon and I do not want them to see me like this."

Barbara looked down at the clothing the army had provided for them. Her homespun dress was so big that it nearly swallowed her whole.

"I am just glad we are not wearing our buckskins!" Barbara said. She glanced at her arms. "I cannot tell you how thankful I am that the walnut juice on my skin has faded. My hair has even lightened again! When Owen and David were reunited with their families, they still looked like young Indian braves."

Barbara thought back to the last day she had seen them. Their families had received Colonel Mercer's message, and when Barbara, Marie, Owen, and David had arrived at

Fort Carlisle, one hundred and forty miles east of Fort Pitt, the boys' families were eagerly waiting there for them.

It was sad to say good-bye. And the sight of their loved ones hugging them in a warm embrace made her even more eager to hear from her mother and brother. "Do you think you will be able to find surviving family members?" Barbara asked Marie with deep concern.

"Yes," Marie said confidently. "I have had over three years to accept the fact that my parents are in heaven. I saw the Indians kill them. But I feel sure I will find my dear aunt and uncle. They told me at Fort Pitt that the Indian raids had not affected their settlement." Marie smiled and grasped Barbara's hand. "The thought of being reunited with them goes far beyond my loveliest dreams."

"It is strange that you have so much confidence, considering that you have not heard a word from them. But somehow I understand your optimism. I have not doubted even for a second that my mother and brother are still alive." Barbara smiled. "I do long to see them. Sometimes I think I cannot bear to wait another second."

The wagon turned and bumped down a side street lined with blossoming cherry trees. Just then a sunbeam broke through the clouds and lit the lane until the pink blossoms glistened. Barbara caught her breath.

"It is beautiful, isn't it?" Marie said as she glanced at her friend.

But Barbara was no longer looking at the cherry blossoms. Her attention was totally focused on the livery stables at the end of the lane. There stood an attractive, gray-haired woman who was staring back at Barbara. From a distance, the woman looked familiar, but Barbara could not be sure.

The woman put her hands over her mouth and rushed toward the wagon. "Barbara!" she cried.

"Mother?" Barbara's words caught in her throat. "Can—can it be?"

"Barbara!" the woman called again with tears streaming down her face. "Oh! It *is* you!"

Barbara did not wait for the officer to stop the wagon. She jumped down and ran into her mother's open arms. "Mother ..." Barbara wrapped her arms tightly around her mother and let her tears flow.

So much had happened since the day over three years earlier when she had last bid her mother farewell. All at once she felt like a little girl again. Her mother was there to soothe all the pain and pent-up emotions she had carried for so long.

"Hello there!" A tall young man approached.

Barbara wiped the tears out of her eyes so she could see clearly.

He shyly asked, "Remember me?"

"John!" She threw her arms around her brother's neck. "I did not recognize you with that beard." John chuckled as he grasped her waist and swung her around in a circle just like when she was little.

"*I* have changed?" John asked with a twinkle in his blue eyes that reminded Barbara of her father. "You are the one who grew up and changed."

"Just look at her, John!" Mother said. "I always told you she would be tall and beautiful." She tenderly brushed back a wisp of Barbara's blond hair. "The message we received said you would not arrive until next week." Looking up at John, Mother smiled. "But I knew you would be here sooner, and John was good enough to let me follow my instinct and come now."

"We have just arrived ourselves." John nodded toward the livery stables. "I have not even unhitched the horses."

"Oh dear!" Barbara cried. "I forgot all about Marie." Turning around, she motioned for Marie to come join the little group. "Mother, you remember our neighbor, Marie LeRoy."

"Of course I do!" Mother embraced Marie with the same motherly love Barbara had missed so much.

The little group headed back to the livery stables and then to find lodging. The baffled young militia escort went to headquarters to report his arrival. Although Barbara felt a little clumsy and awkward in the large dress the army had supplied, she soon felt as if she had never been gone.

It was a wonderfully perfect day—perfect, that is, in every way but one. Barbara's heart sank when she learned Mother had not heard a word of Regina. It pained her deeply to tell her mother she and Regina had been separated over three years earlier.

"Mother, I tried not to let them take her away—I have done everything I can to find her. I feel sure Regina is still alive." Barbara's words did little to ease the look of pain on her mother's face.

123

She patted her daughter's hand. "Of course you have done everything you can—that is just like my Barbara to be so concerned for her little sister's well-being." Mother wrapped her arms around Barbara's waist and gazed into her eyes. "But nothing can dampen the joy of seeing you. God willing, we will soon rejoice in Regina's return as well."

<hr />

Their stay in Philadelphia did not last long. John had to get back to the farm. But before they left, Mother insisted on buying material to make Barbara some dresses. John said he had some shopping to do too, but nothing could have prepared Barbara for their surprise. Her eyes grew wide when John presented her with a lovely blue Sunday dress. It was the same one she had seen in the shop window with the delicate lace and pleats.

"Oh, John! It's beautiful!" Barbara exclaimed. "Once I put on this dress, no one will be able to guess I have just returned from the wilderness." Barbara ran her fingers across the fine pleats and tucks. "Wherever did you get the money?"

"I had some stashed away for a special time." John grinned with satisfaction. "Besides, I do not have a wife or sweetheart, and I cannot think of anyone else I would rather spend it on—I have prayed for three and a half years for an opportunity like this."

<hr />

Marie received word from her relatives shortly before the Leiningers headed home. Her family had moved to a settlement in Maryland, just outside of the Pennsylvania Territory. Knowing Marie would soon be with her own family helped to ease the ache in Barbara's heart when it came time to say good-bye. They had been through so much together. It seemed strange that they had to part. Marie tried to act strong, but Barbara knew her too well. She saw Marie's swollen eyes.

"Good-bye, my dear friend." Barbara wrapped her arms around Marie's shoulders. "Promise me you will write as soon as you are settled. Mother and John live in the town of Tulpehocken. It is much closer to Philadelphia than Penn's Creek, so it will not take as long for the mail to travel."

Marie nodded, and Barbara could tell a knot in her throat kept her from saying anything. "We *will* see each other again. I know we will," Barbara said. "Mother says the road between there and Tulpehocken is good. Maybe you can come visit us sometime." Barbara hugged her friend one last time.

John helped Marie into the wagon. She waved until they rounded the corner and Marie was out of sight. Barbara turned and looked at the road ahead. Her emotions were mixed. She would miss her friend dearly, yet there was nowhere else she would rather be than sitting between Mother and John. She was finally going home!

Mother understood. She wrapped her arm around Barbara and whispered, "You are almost home!"

Chapter 14

FIVE YEARS LATER

*B*arbara listened to the rain's soft patter through the open doorway as she quietly stoked the dying embers in the hearth. She had just begun the tedious job of making cheese and needed to melt the curds and whey. John had built a good fire before breakfast, but that had been hours ago. He had gone into the township of Tulpehocken to buy seed for spring planting. Their widowed neighbor had taken ill, and Mother had gone to care for her. That left Barbara alone on the farm. She did not mind, especially on days like these.

Breathing deeply of the rain-scented breeze that filtered through the doorway as she looked out, Barbara watched the delicate raindrops bathe the budding world about her. She always loved rainy days, but today the soothing tones combined with the solitude caused her to remember their old cabin along Penn's Creek. At first

Barbara had been saddened to learn that her mother and John had left their old Pennsylvania homestead to settle farther east near Philadelphia. She missed the home where her whole family had last been together. But, as the years passed without any sign or word of Regina, Barbara knew Penn's Creek was the last place she wanted to be. A constant reminder of the days she and Regina had played along the creek banks would be far too painful.

Barbara sighed as she lifted the iron kettle and set the handle on the large hook that extended above the flames. It had been eight and a half years since she had last seen Regina. Barbara thought of her every day. Mother often mentioned her name, and John prayed for her daily before the evening meal.

Barbara stooped over the hearth, stirring the curds and watching them slowly crumble as the whey dissolved into steam. She smiled as she thought of her own homecoming and how hard it had been to adjust to civilized farm life after three and a half years in the wilderness. Compared to her buckskins, the many cumbersome layers of her dresses made her feel hampered. In the summer, she felt confined cooking over a hearth instead of out in the open air. And sleeping on soft bedding still felt odd even after experiencing it again at the fort. Many times, long after Mother and John were asleep, Barbara would slip out of bed and lie on the hard wooden floor. Barbara laughed at the memories of how awkward she had felt.

The townsfolk had been fascinated by her story, and she could scarcely go anywhere without being the center of attention. She was always afraid she would trip on her petticoat or, without thinking, kick off her tight, stiff shoes. Thankfully, she had adjusted and soon felt completely at ease in town and actually enjoyed participating in the church socials.

A shadow passed over Barbara's face when she thought of these weekly gatherings. She placed the kettle on the wood table and salted the moist crumbled curd. She loved the church socials, but the sweet memories were mixed with pain.

John's best friend, Peter Ruffner, had been a true friend to Barbara since the first day she had arrived home. He and John were about the same age, and both had blond hair—only Peter's was curly. Peter spent many evenings in their home and joined her family at every social. He and John watched over her like a hawk. Anytime she felt slightly uncomfortable or found herself in an awkward position, Peter always seemed to know, and somehow he made everything right. As the years passed, John and Peter continued to watch over her—only then it was to keep eager young suitors far away. At first Barbara wondered if she would ever marry. But then she realized that her happiest hours were spent with the two of them; she enjoyed no others in the world more. Of course, she loved her brother, but she realized she loved Peter too—as a brother. At least that's what she told herself. She did not—she could not—love him more than that.

He was a good man, who attended church from time to time. But Peter did not understand the full meaning of being a Christian. To him, Christianity was just a form of religion—a moral and social practice. He and John spent many hours talking about loving God with your whole heart and living a life committed to Christ. But Peter never seemed to fully understand. This grieved Barbara, and she spent many hours praying for his salvation. She longed for him to know the depth of Christ's love the same way she did. Still, Barbara had convinced herself that she only cared for him as a brother. But now the full reality of how much she truly loved Peter had become apparent to her.

Barbara sighed. She looked out the doorway again and watched the rain for some time before pouring the curds into a large basket lined with cheesecloth. The memory brought back a pain that stabbed her heart every time she thought of it, yet Barbara was convinced she had made the right decision.

John had come to her one evening. Before he even spoke a word, Barbara could tell by his heavy brow and intense yet caring eyes that something was on his mind. She remembered the sick feeling that grew in her stomach when John had looked at her and said, "I talked with Peter today." The sound of Mother's spinning wheel stopped and Barbara knew what John was going to say.

"That's nice," Barbara said nonchalantly. "Is he well?"

"He couldn't be better," John said. "He has just purchased some acreage in New Holland, about fifteen miles from here." John shifted uneasily. "He plans to have a cabin built before winter."

Barbara's face flushed to a deep crimson.

Then John proceeded to say what Barbara hoped for and feared at the same time. Peter loved her and had asked John's blessing to marry her. John went on to say that he and Mother wanted to hear what was in Barbara's heart before giving an answer.

That night Barbara had retreated to her room. She wanted to be alone with the Lord. She knew she loved Peter dearly. She would always love him, but Barbara also knew she could not marry a man who did not share her faith. Finally, after a night spent in heartfelt tears, Barbara gave Mother and John her answer. Although they too loved Peter and were saddened by the situation, they both confirmed her decision. Mother had encouraged Barbara, saying that perhaps it just was not the right timing. Perhaps God would change Peter's heart and give him an understanding of his Savior.

That had been a year ago and nothing had changed. Only now Peter lived fifteen miles away, and she had not seen him all winter. Peter had promised John he would come to help him during spring planting, but Barbara was not sure if Peter would ever want to see her again.

Barbara shook her head. "It *was* the right decision!" she declared aloud. By now, most of the whey had drained from the curds. Securing the top of the cheesecloth, Barbara squeezed the excess moisture. *If I had wanted to marry an unsaved man, I could have married Galasko,* she thought. After folding the cheesecloth tightly around the drained curds, she put it in the cupboard and placed a large, flat stone on top of it to start the curing process. *Only, I did not love Galasko.* Barbara wiped her hands on her gray, soiled apron. She knew there was only one man she could ever love, and she would just have to wait and pray—no matter how many years went by.

When John returned from town that evening, he was not alone. Barbara was almost finished milking the cow when she saw the two riders coming up the lane. She recognized John's horse right away, but because of the drizzle, she could not distinguish the other rider.

"Dear me!" Barbara looked down at her muddy apron and bare feet. "If I had known company was coming, I would have worn my shoes and pressed my good apron." She brushed a loose strand of hair out of her eye and tried to milk faster.

"Come on, Clover," she urged soothingly to the cow. "We cannot let our company see a lady of the house in such a fashion." But John and his guest arrived before Barbara was finished.

"Good evening!" Barbara heard a familiar voice above her.

Stunned, Barbara looked up. Her heart froze and the color drained out of her cheeks. Peter was leaning over Clover's back, grinning down at her. His big green eyes were full of amusement.

"Where did you come from?" Barbara tried to hide her bare feet under her milking stool. "I mean, why did— how did you manage to get here through the rain?" She could feel her heart beating faster, and the drained color began to flush back into her cheeks.

Peter chuckled and his smile broadened, defining the dimple in his chin. "I came all this way to tell you — your whole family — something. I came through the rain because I could not wait another day."

Barbara could only imagine what he was going to say. But she kept her heart in check.

"Barbara, I want you to know I have put my faith in Jesus Christ and in him alone. I now know it is not enough to just be a good person. Religion without the cleansing power of Jesus' blood is useless." Peter paused. "I finally understand the depth of his love for me — that he would lay down his life for my salvation. I now see the love that motivates you to sacrifice all for the sake of Christ."

All of a sudden, Barbara did not mind that she was barefoot, and she forgot she was covered in mud. She looked up at Peter, and her eyes filled with tears. She did not need to say anything — she knew Peter understood.

Peter grew serious. "There is something else I must tell you."

Barbara could not believe what she was hearing. Could it be that he still loved her?

"You see, when I told my parents about my newfound faith, they did not understand. They did not understand at all. In fact ..."

Barbara's mind began to spin. How foolish she had been. Here she thought he still loved her, but he was just treating her like an old friend—like his little sister. Barbara felt her face grow hot as she tried to regain her composure and focus on what Peter was saying.

" ... they even wrote me out of their will."

Barbara caught her breath. "I am so sorry," she said, hoping he had not read her previous thoughts. Now she truly felt ashamed. "You know you are always welcome here. But—but that isn't the same, is it?" she stammered.

Peter gazed into Barbara's eyes. "No, you are right; it is not quite the same."

Barbara looked away, trying not to appear hurt.

"Barbara," he said, "it is not the same because this home has captured a special place in my heart no other home can fill." Peter shifted nervously. Then, taking Barbara's hand in his, he said, "Barbara, could I ever hope to have your heart? I've always loved you—ever since you came back a shy, awkward fifteen-year-old. I already wrote your mother and John. They have given me their—"

"Yes!" Barbara could not wait another second. "My answer is yes!"

Barbara and Peter were married six months later beneath the golden glow of an autumn sky. Barbara thought her heart would nearly burst with joy. But a cloud shadowed the glories of the day. That autumn marked the passage of nine years since the Penn's Creek massacre that had forever changed their world. Even though it was her wedding day, Barbara got a faraway look in her eyes as she gazed at the western horizon. Deep within her heart she knew Regina was still alive and longed to have her share this special day with her.

Chapter 15

THE SONG OF MY HEART

*B*arbara loved being married and diligently labored to turn their new house into a home. She knew Peter adored her. At first, life was so busy with fall harvest that Barbara looked forward to the winter months when things would slow down and they could spend more time together. She helped Peter in the fields whenever she could, but many household duties came along with the title of Mrs. Ruffner. The only time she saw Peter during the afternoon was when she took him water out in the field. Often, he was so weary at night that he would fall into bed after supper, too tired to stay up and talk by the hearth, as they loved to do.

She also looked forward to winter because she and Peter planned to visit Mother and John for Christmas.

Now that she and Peter lived fifteen miles from her family, they were not able to visit as often. As the long, hard days of harvest passed, Barbara anticipated seeing her mother. She sensed this Christmas would be special for all of them.

Christmas Eve came at last. Barbara did not mind the long trip. She loved the sounds of the clanking harness and the soft thud of the horses' hooves landing on the hard-packed snow. But, best of all, Mother and John were waiting on the other side of the long journey. When they swished around the bend and drove up to the cabin, Mother was eagerly waiting at the window with a candle. Its glow illuminated the sweet smile on her face. Barbara's heart filled with joy.

Mother rushed to the door and swung it wide open. "Welcome home and merry Christmas!" she said with her deep German accent. Her hair had grayed over the years, but her heart still shone bright with love. After embracing her daughter and new son-in-law, she ushered them out of the cold and into the kitchen. "You have come at last and just in time—"

She would have finished if it were not for John. He was stoking the fire as they entered the kitchen. Smiling, he filled in the rest of his mother's sentence.

"Yes, supper could not have waited much longer ..." Then, with a twinkle in his blue eyes he gave his sister a hug and added, " ... and neither could I."

Supper truly was delightful. They had so much to catch up on. It seemed like years since they had last seen each other instead of just a few short months. Barbara beamed over the praise Peter lavished on her as he told Mother what a wonderful daughter she had raised and the fine wife she had become.

Dinner went far into the evening, and fellowship around the hearth continued on even longer. John put log after log on the fire, and before long they realized they were in the middle of a snowstorm. The gusty winds had picked up, and the little snowflakes that once delicately danced about the sky now swirled and fell with such fierceness that the whole world seemed to be caught in its freezing grip.

Just then there was a loud knock on the door. For a moment everyone froze, wondering what could motivate someone to venture out on a night like this—and on Christmas Eve too. John and Peter jumped to their feet and rushed to the door.

"Why, Reverend Muhlenburg!" John exclaimed. "What would bring you here on such a night? Is your family well?"

The poor man was too cold to answer. The men quickly led the reverend to the fire while Barbara hurried to boil some water for tea to warm his insides.

After being sufficiently warmed, the kind old parson finally spoke.

"When I started out earlier this evening, I had no idea the weather would turn like this, but I have news that cannot wait." He paused, a joyful look on his face.

Barbara began to fear he might never get to the news.

At last he looked directly at her mother and said, "Colonel Bouquet has signed a treaty with the Indians that has freed all the white captives."

Barbara caught her breath and glanced at her mother. Despite the warm glow of the fire, her mother's face had gone completely pale.

"I have reason to believe that, if your daughter Regina is still alive, she would be among the two hundred and six captives the colonel has escorted to Fort Carlisle."

"Oh, Reverend!" Mother Leininger grasped his hand in gratefulness. "Thank you! You have risked so much to tell us this news, and we cannot adequately express our gratitude." She turned to John. "We must leave as soon as possible." Her face slowly sobered and a tear trickled down her cheek as she spoke softly to the reverend. "I hope … and yet, I fear to hope Regina is still alive. You see, I have been praying for nine years that I would see my baby girl again—if I were to go and not find her, I fear it would be too difficult."

The reverend took her hand in his. "Faith is the substance of things hoped for, the evidence of things not seen." He smiled confidently. "There is good reason to hope, and besides, God delights in giving good gifts to his children."

Barbara lay awake most of the night, thinking and praying that their journey to Fort Carlisle would end in a joyous reunion. Tears ran down her cheeks as she thought of the last night she and Regina had been together. She remembered how frightened her little sister had been as they slept out under the stars with the Indians standing guard. She remembered how she had wrapped her arms around Regina and assured her that no matter what happened, God would always be with her. Barbara gained a glimmer of hope as she recalled how Regina had snuggled deeper into her arms and promised she would never lose the song in her heart. But that was so long ago—a different life in a different land.

"Is it possible that she could remember her native language?" Barbara wondered. "Does she still trust God and have his Word hidden in her heart? Did she remember her promise?" She had heard of captives who completely forgot their former lives, even their own families. All these thoughts swirled through Barbara's mind as she drifted into a fitful sleep.

By morning the snowstorm had gained in intensity, making it impossible to start the sixty-mile journey to Fort Carlisle. Finally, after three days, they set out. The harsh winter winds and freezing climate made their travel long and tedious, but they at last arrived at the fort the afternoon of New Year's Eve in 1764. Barbara and her mother reported immediately to Colonel Bouquet at the army outpost while the men saw to the horses and found lodging for the night.

The sight of over two hundred captives dressed in native garb brought a flood of memories back to Barbara. The smell of their buckskins mixed with the strong scent of campfire smoke gave her the feeling she was once again in the Indian village.

Barbara and her mother anxiously searched each face as they walked down the long rows of captives. Many turned their heads in fear or looked at the ground in confusion. Some had walnut-stained skin just like Barbara's had been. Others looked so pale that they almost blended with the snow. Some were thin and sickly from their long journey.

Barbara wanted to wrap them in her arms and tell them she understood what they had been through, and that the worst was over—everything was going to be all right. She saw captives of all ages, but there was no sign of Regina.

"The poor dears," her mother finally cried. "They look so confused—so frightened."

Barbara remembered how she anxiously, yet fearfully, looked forward to meeting the English at Fort Pitt. "You must remember, Mother," Barbara said reassuringly, "that some of them have not seen white people in over nine years. I was a little nervous at first too." Barbara so wanted to encourage her mother. But as she looked at the disheveled group, she wondered if they would be able to recognize Regina. After all, she would now be eighteen— a young Indian woman.

Mother approached someone who seemed to be about Regina's age. Speaking softly, she reached for the girl's arm. "Do not fear. I will not harm you."

The girl shrank away in fear.

"Do you know your name, child?" Mother spoke in German, but it was no use. It was evident that she did not understand English or German. The terrified young woman would not even look at Barbara and her mother.

They spoke to several other captives, but their hopes were repeatedly dashed. Finally, Mother turned away with tears in her eyes. "I am afraid we will have to tell Colonel Bouquet that Regina is not here."

Barbara's heart grew sick at the thought of being so close only to leave knowing they could have passed her by.

Mother leaned against Barbara for support. Barbara feared the excitement of possibly finding Regina, followed by the long hard journey, then the discouraging and seemingly impossible search, was all more than the older woman could bear.

It was all Barbara could do to keep from crying. *Dear Lord*, she prayed silently, *after all these years of hoping and praying, please — oh please, lead us to —*

A man's deep voice interrupted her prayer, and she saw her mother looking up at Colonel Bouquet.

"Have you found your daughter?" His face was kind and Barbara could see the care and concern in his eyes.

"No," Mother said in despair. "No, we have not found her."

Barbara could not stand it any longer. She had to say something. "If you please, sir." Barbara curtsied politely, fearing her words an intrusion. "I feel in my heart that my sister is indeed here. But after these nine years, we have no way of recognizing her."

Colonel Bouquet combed his beard with his fingers; his face expressed his deep concern. "Did your sister have any birthmarks?" He turned back to Mother. "Or perhaps your daughter has a childhood scar you could remember her by?"

Barbara's mother shook her head in disappointment. "No, my Regina was a little angel without one mark or blemish."

"Is there a family heirloom she might recognize, like a locket or a trinket of some sort?"

"No, no, none at all. The Indians took most of our valuables during the massacre. What they did not take was lost when they burned our cabin to the ground." Mother's eyes filled with tears. Barbara could tell she was remembering that awful day. Mother had often told her how she and John had heard of the raids and were unsure of their family's safety, but nothing could have prepared them for the loss they returned to. Mother closed her eyes as if to shut out the memory and quickly brushed away the freely flowing tears. Looking back toward the colonel, she took a deep breath and straightened her shoulders with fresh determination.

"I am sorry to hear that," the colonel said with deepest compassion. "I understand that you lost much more that day than just your possessions. Perhaps you will yet be reunited with your daughter." He thought for a moment and then brightened. "Perhaps you can think of a child-hood memory she might have held onto all these years—a term of endearment or a song?"

"Mother! Do you remember how Regina loved to sing, and you used to call her your little songbird?"

Mother nodded and renewed hope shone in her eyes. "Yes—yes, you are right!" she said. "I used to sing 'Alone Yet Not All Alone' to Regina many nights before bed." She smiled wistfully at the colonel. "It was her favorite song."

"That is a perfect memory! Why not walk back through the rows of captives singing that song," Colonel Bouquet urged. "You never know what might trigger her memory."

Such was the depth of her renewed faith and hope that it was all Mother could do to keep her voice controlled as she walked back through the rows of captives. Barbara followed quietly, mouthing the words behind her.

I am with Him and He with me
Even here alone I cannot be.

Barbara listened as her mother's sweet voice warmed the cold winter air. She watched the faces of the captives as they passed, and though many seemed comforted by her mother's calming tones, none were especially moved.

Suddenly, Barbara heard a loud cry! A tall, slender girl rushed toward her mother.

Could it be Regina? But then Barbara noticed a younger girl following the tall girl, so she thought it must not be her sister. Then Barbara stared in disbelief; her mother was embracing the tall girl.

Next, the most amazing thing happened—her mother and the girl were singing the song together. It *was* Regina!

Tears of joy filled Barbara's eyes as she stumbled toward her mother and sister, blinded by her tears. She reached them just in time to hear their voices blending as they sang the last verse of Regina's song.

When the song ended and Barbara was able to see through her tears, she looked deep into Regina's blue eyes and could still see the sparkle that had always brightened their days. With a cry of joy, Barbara and Regina embraced and held each other for a long time. Amazingly enough, Barbara knew that in their spirits, they had never been apart.

It was some time before Regina ventured to communicate in the only language she could speak fluently—the Iroquoian tongue. With tears of joy and a voice full of emotion, she whispered in Barbara's ear:

"I remembered my promise. I never lost the song of my heart!"

CONCLUSION

*A*n additional blessing came with the Leiningers' joyous reunion: the orphaned girl, Susanna, who had been given to Regina after the Indian raid.

The Indians had allowed Regina to care for and raise the child throughout the years of her captivity. She took the responsibility seriously for one so young. She taught Susanna to trust in the Lord Jesus Christ—the God of her fathers. When they were in the woods together, far from the earshot of their master, Regina would sing "Alone, Yet Not All Alone" to her little charge, until she too loved to sing of her Savior's great love.

Susanna's parents had been killed in the massacre. No surviving relatives were found, so Mother Leininger gladly welcomed the young girl into her heart and home.

Soon Regina and Mrs. Leininger's reunion was known far and wide. Shortly after her return, Regina, who only remembered a few words in German, asked her mother if they could visit Reverend Henry Muhlenburg and to see, in Regina's words, "God's book that Father used to read to me."

It was a long journey, but on February 2, 1765, Mrs. Leininger and her daughter arrived at Reverend Muhlenburg's home in Germantown. He was both astonished and delighted when the young woman reverently opened his German Bible and read numerous passages. Though she had forgotten most of her native language, she had hidden God's Word in her heart at a young age and never forgotten it. Regina could both read and recite from memory the verses and hymns she learned before her captivity.

Reverend Muhlenburg's heart was so touched by this young woman of unwavering faith that he gave her the Bible she loved so dearly. He also wrote to his home church in Germany, telling them the story and encouraging them to teach their children about the power of the Living Word exemplified by this family.

Barbara and her husband continued to live a peaceful and full life on their farm. They were blessed with four children. Barbara died in 1805 and is buried in the Allegheny Reformed Church Cemetery in Brecknock Township.

Regina never married, but lived contentedly with her mother, helping to raise her adopted sister, Susanna, and serving those around her. She was known throughout the community for her kindness and willingness to lay down her life for others.

Regina is buried beside her mother at Christ Evangelical Lutheran Church just outside of Stouchsburg in Berks County, Pennsylvania.

AUTHOR'S NOTE

My grandmother Leininger first told me the story of Barbara and Regina after coming across the account while studying our family's genealogy. That was years ago, yet the story continues to make a strong impression on my heart, impacting and inspiring me to this day.

My first draft of *Alone Yet Not Alone* was written when I was nine years old. Of course, the content has changed dramatically since that time. But one thing has never changed—the picture of two young sisters torn from family during their tender years. Despite all obstacles, they do not forsake their faith in Jesus Christ and never "lose the song of their hearts."

It is my prayer that those reading this book will be encouraged to run the race of life with undaunted faith and endurance—drawing strength from the author and finisher of our faith, Jesus Christ.

DISCUSSION QUESTIONS

1. What is the name of the historical attack in which Barbara and Regina were taken captive?

2. What was the name of the Indian tribe which captured the sisters?

3. How are the sisters in the story related to the author?

4. A story that is told orally and passed down from one person to another is an example of what kind of literature?

5. What was used to dye Barbara's skin and hair?

6. Why was it so risky for Barbara and the others to attempt an escape?

7. How many years had passed from their capture to Barbara's escape?

8. How many years had passed until they found Regina?

9. Why do you think Regina wasn't able to speak up when her family was looking for her among the captives?

10. Do you have a family story to share?

We want to hear from you. Please send your comments about this book to us in care of zreview@zondervan.com. Thank you.

ZONDERVAN.com/
AUTHORTRACKER
follow your favorite authors